The Heart and Soul of
LANDON
By Helen Godfrey Pyke
HARRIS

Helen Godfrey Pyke

1993

The Heart and Soul of LANDON HARRIS

By Helen Godfrey Pyke

REVIEW AND HERALD® PUBLISHING ASSOCIATION
HAGERSTOWN, MD 21740

The author assumes full responsibility for the accuracy of all facts and quotations
as cited in this book.

This book was
Edited by Penny Estes Wheeler
Designed by Byron Steele
Cover art by John Edens
Typeset: 11/12 Isabel Book

PRINTED IN U.S.A.

96 95 94 93 92 91   10 9 8 7 6 5 4 3 2 1

Library of Congress Cataloging-in-Publication Data
Pyke, Helen Godfrey.
    The heart and soul of Landon Harris / Helen Godfrey Pyke.
        p.   cm.
    1. Harris, Landon. 2. Seventh-day Adventists—United States—Biography.
I. Title.
BX6193.H315P94   1991
286.7'092—dc20
[B]
                                                        90-19399
                                                        CIP

ISBN 0-8280-0596-6

Contents

PART ONE

LANDON HARRIS gulped half a glassful of iced tea, set his glass down, and looked around Hallivand Steel Company's atrium lunch room. The tea settled in his stomach like a fistful of ice cubes. He shivered.

"I'm a rational person," he told himself even as his imagination recreated the dream which had haunted him for nearly two weeks.

Landon knew that the dream was nothing more than his brain's response to emotional overload. It was a mistake to watch that TV evangelist when he was so tired. Furthermore, he should never have gone to bed on two servings of stroganoff. All week at work—in the elevator, in his office, here in the lunch room—it was as if his brain kept hitting the REPLAY switch on a video simulation program, and like the voice of Armageddon itself, the evangelist intoned, *"Babylon is fallen, is fallen, that great city."* Landon felt smothered in the rubble of Chicago, not knowing for certain if there had been an earthquake or a fire or a flood—possibly a nuclear attack. Or maybe the whole system had collapsed upon itself, under the weight of its data banks, its information systems, its power structure. In the dream he was aware that he was not alone. When he stirred in the crumbled concrete, turning his face in the dust of plaster, in the rubble near him he always heard another person cough then groan against the small sounds of plaster still falling from somewhere and the noise of water gushing from a broken pipe.

Landon Harris was still staring and was startled when Peggy came with her tray.

"Mind if I have lunch with you?" she asked, settling the end of the tray on the back of the chair.

"Sure. Why not?" Landon said. He stood and held the tray for her while she placed her food on the table.

"There was a long line today," Peggy said. "I'll have to hurry to get back to my office before 1:15. How you been, Landon?"

Landon glanced around the lunch room then let his eyes settle on Peggy's neat bronze-colored hands buttering her roll, setting her knife down, bringing the roll to her mouth.

"I'm doing fine," he said. "Only just not quite satisfied in spite of the facts." He smiled, wondering if Peggy knew about Diana, if by any chance Diana had been by her office this week. Wondered what she might have said.

"I saw you with the boys at the public library last Saturday," Peggy said. "You were just leaving Science and Technology as I looked up from the terminal I was using. I would have said something if you hadn't been so far away."

Landon had nearly finished his meal, but he had no reason to rush back to his office. Things were a lot more flexible in engineering than in the other departments of Hallivand Steel Company. Officially he was working out a major structural defect—a stress factor in the steel supports of a company warehouse in Albany. And right now the whole problem needed to incubate for a while. It was about the same issue that he had visited the library, looking for a microfilmed copy of November's *Men and Steel*.

"Do you still have Robbie on the weekends?" Peggy asked, a shrimp poised on her fork. Her eyes were curious, but not too curious, Landon decided.

"Alternate weekends," he said. "His mother takes him upstate to spend Saturdays with her parents quite a bit."

Landon wondered what Diana had said about their separation and the impending disaster he perceived to be coming.

"You're not very talkative," Peggy said, her smile moving slowly from her lips to the dimples that appeared in her cheeks when the smile was full. Landon wadded up the paper napkin in his hand and pushed it into the empty tea glass.

"I guess not," he said. "No offense meant, Peggy."

He saw that she was ready to leave and rose himself, but sat back down as she turned from the table toward the escalator that would take her two stories up to the mezzanine where she worked as private secretary to a company executive. He watched her going up, her back rigid, her hand on the moving rail. She must have had something to say to him but decided not to say it. Probably something Diana had told her. He was tired. Too tired to care what Diana had said or what Peggy thought. His eyes traveled to the top of the escalator with Peggy, then moved on up the several stories beyond the mezzanine to the patch of sky, blue even through the smoke-tinted glass overhead.

It's probably 95 degrees outside, he thought. Tomorrow it would be too hot to take the boys to the boat show as he had planned. They would be disappointed. Of course, if Diana would agree to it, he might take them in the late afternoon on into the evening. If Diana would agree. If Diana would agree to anything these days. He dreaded even calling her about plans for the weekend. But that was just the price he had to pay if he wanted to see Ryan. She didn't have to let him see the boy at all.

Landon pushed his chair back finally and crossed the

dining room to the elevators in the front lobby. He got off on the eleventh floor—actually the top floor—above the sophisticated confusion of the company's chief operations where the nitty-gritty stuff took place, where the planners and dreamers soared or groveled, one or the other, dealing with the problems on which the entire company depended.

The eleventh floor was one vast open space with temporary partitions set up in a roughly grid-like pattern. Where he got off the elevator, the corridors led away like main arteries to branch into narrower corridors. Landon set off briskly to the left, turning right where an arrow pointed toward Stress Control. He turned left at the water cooler then left again where a poster urged employees to donate blood to the local blood bank. His cubicle was the second on the right. Since the company encouraged employees to individualize work areas, he had pinned a Gone Fishing sign on the pearl gray fabric of the divider. His work area had no door, but when he went inside, he had quite a bit of privacy, for his desk was against the outer wall, around the corner and out of sight of people passing by.

Landon switched on his computer and spoke into the identifying device which gave him access to his files. The problem on which he had been working for the past month came up, the equations confronting him with the same puzzling probabilities. Around him the noises of the eleventh floor intensified as more of the engineers returned from their lunch hour, and Landon sank into the hum and buzz of thought that would carry him through until 5:00.

Landon imagined the heat he would encounter when he emerged from the elevated passage which crossed the street from Hallivand Steel's high-rise office building to the parking ramp. The tinted glass arching over the passage gave him the sensation of walking some kind of tightrope strung between the two buildings, not so high up as to terrify the performer, but high enough that traffic below seemed unimportant. Although the passage was air-conditioned,

Landon felt perspiration beading his forehead, and the hair at the back of his neck was damp.

He stepped into the down elevator at the end of the crossover and pressed the button for Level Three where he always parked. He would pick Robbie up at the Y where he would just have finished his swimming practice. His son's dark hair would be wet against his head, and his lips still blue from being in the cold water too long. Robbie would ask about Ryan. What was there to say?

The elevator stopped. Landon got off and headed for his dark blue sedan. Ryan would still be at the library where he was enrolled in the summer reading program. Robbie would want to know why they couldn't just drive by and pick him up the way they usually did on Friday afternoons.

At the bottom of the ramp Landon handed the attendant his parking pass, watched him run it through the scanner, then took it back.

"Evening, Mr. Harris," the attendant said.

The light turned green, and Landon drove out into the street, grateful that the air conditioner was beginning to cool the interior of the car even though the steering wheel was still hot in his hands.

I ought to just do it, he thought. Diana wouldn't come from wherever she shopped until at least 6:30. The boys could have a half hour together before she came for Ryan herself. If she remembered. Nearly from the beginning of their marriage four years ago, he had been the one to pick up her son, wherever he was, at day care, at the school, at summer day camp. At first he did it because looking out for Ryan made it easier for him being separated from Robbie so much, but after a while, when the two boys became friends, and when he and Ryan had spent a lot of time together, it was as if he was really Ryan's father.

Ryan, how can I give you up?

Tears blurred the traffic ahead, and he brushed his hand across his eyes.

Twenty minutes later, with Robbie in the car, Landon explained the situation. "We may not have a chance to see Ryan very often from now on, son. Should we run by and see him at least?"

Robbie seemed not to understand.

"Do you mean when you and Diana get a divorce, you can't keep getting Ryan on Saturdays the way you get me? How come?"

"I'm your father," Landon said. "I'm not Ryan's real father."

"I don't see what difference it makes," Robbie said.

Landon guessed that an 8-year-old couldn't be expected to grasp the fine points of divorce laws or even the broader conventions of family relations and the patterns by which these relationships fragmented.

"Let's drop by the library for just a few minutes," he said.

"Yes," Robbie agreed.

Seeing the two boys together, knowing that they had just a half hour before Diana might make her appearance, gave Landon an unsteady feeling in his vitals. He watched Ryan lay out the four books he had checked out. It was surprising, he pondered, how much the boys actually looked alike, both of them blue-eyed with similar hair styles, both with a studious look about the mouth that was surprising in boys of their age . . . the way they stood, the way they walked, the way they looked up when someone spoke to them.

Now as the librarian's assistant to whose group Ryan belonged came by their table, Ryan touched her arm. "This is Robbie, my brother."

"Oh," she said. "Then you must be twins."

"And this is my dad," Ryan said.

"Hello, Mr. Andrews," the woman said.

"Hello," he said, letting it pass.

Ryan's face remained grave, but when the woman left the table, he winked a slow, sober wink at Robbie and then at Landon. Robbie winked back.

Startled, he realized they both imitated his own mannerisms.

The boys restacked the books, both of them glancing at the clock.

"Do you think she remembered?" Ryan asked him.

"No doubt," Landon said. He hesitated.

"Just to be safe, we'll circulate for a while in Fine Arts," he said. "Architecture. Then if she doesn't show by 7:30, you send someone over to find me. We won't leave until we know for sure you're OK."

Ryan grinned and he and Robbie pinched each other on the arm and winked again.

"Thanks," Ryan said.

Robbie was satisfied listening to a tape with one of the headsets, and Landon sat down with *Thirty Early Scottish Castles* at an adjoining table from which he could keep his eye on the entrance to the children's reading room. He could guess how frightened Ryan was, thrown as he was so suddenly into the unknown. Landon hated Diana for what she had done to Ryan. He was almost disappointed when he saw her go in, and pained in a new and terrifying way as he watched her leave with her son.

Diana Melton Andrews Rogers Harris, he thought. *A beautiful lady. Impressive. Brilliant. Not actually charming. Something more austere than charming. Leave it at impressive.* Ryan walked beside her, talking steadily but not holding her hand the way Robbie held Joetta's hand when they went somewhere together. Just as they turned to step into the elevator, she looked his way, her face impassive, alert. He hoped she didn't notice him peering around the large book about castles.

"Let's go," he told Robbie.

He was hardly settled yet in the apartment. It was the first time Robbie had seen it.

"Where's my room?" Robbie asked when they entered the living room.

"Do you mind sharing a room with me?" Landon asked him.

He led the way to the bedroom.

"Oh, twin beds," Robbie said. He set his duffle bag on the floor and opened the closet door.

"Your things are on the left," Landon told him. "And you can move into the smaller chest of drawers."

"Is this my stuff?" Robbie asked, thumping a box marked Prime Florida Tomatoes.

Saturday they slept late then went out for breakfast about 11:00. They spent the afternoon in the coolness of the mall theater watching cartoons. They ate out again afterward before returning to the apartment.

"Why don't you cook something?" Robbie asked as he put a half gallon of milk in the refrigerator.

"I haven't stocked the kitchen yet," Landon said. He opened a cabinet door. "Three margarine bowls and a package of paper cups. Oh, and I do have a handful of plastic spoons and one small skillet."

Robbie was surprised when Landon suggested on Sunday morning that they attend church.

"Which church?"

"I've never been to a Catholic church," Landon said. "Shall we try that one? I'm not really a connoisseur of churches. I just thought . . ."

He didn't mention that last Sunday he had gone alone to a Baptist church on Seventh Street. After that terrible dream.

During the organ prelude and during the choral introit, he watched his son's face, trying to guess the child's response to the deep vibrations, the strong resonances he felt as he listened.

The Wednesday before Landon was to have Robbie for the weekend again, Joetta phoned.

"I hope you don't mind taking Rob to the doctor on Saturday morning," she said. "He's been having a sore throat, and that's the earliest appointment I could get."

She gave him the doctor's name and the office location. "Rob said you took him to church," she said.

"I hope you don't mind," Landon said, and realized that he had echoed her tone of voice as well as her trite half-apology.

"No, I was just a little surprised."

Landon smiled to himself. He guessed she would be. He had hardly acted in character.

Thursday he went to a Woolworth's to pick up a set of plastic dishes and some flatware, both service for four, which would be all right if they washed dishes after each second meal, he decided. He got a pitcher for mixing orange juice and two sauce pans. At the supermarket he bought the basics so that he could really cook something, also a few of the packaged meals with everything included in one box.

Friday evening he and Robbie fixed a Chinese supper complete with fortune cookies and an exotic herbal tea.

"I like this better than eating out," Robbie said.

"Me too," Landon admitted.

Saturday morning, in spite of the appointment which Joetta had made for 11:30, they had to wait to see the doctor. Landon shuffled the stack of magazines on the table in the waiting room. From appearances, most of the adults bringing children to this pediatrician were women. He finally picked one of the more general women's magazines and sat down. Leafing through it, he stopped at an article called "Surviving the Trauma of Divorce." He glanced at Robbie, settled beside him with a book. He noticed it was Bible stories.

"Hmmm," he mused. Maybe they should try church again tomorrow.

Last week, by himself, he had attended a Presbyterian church. He wondered if Robbie would like to return to the

Catholic church or if they should shop around a bit.

The author of the divorce article mentioned several points which Landon thought significant but did not discuss dealing with separation from step-children. *Obviously, Landon thought, people, while they could be excused for messing up one marriage, were not supposed to need a second divorce. Obviously, they should learn from their first experience.*

Growth. That was the word. Divorce was supposed to offer opportunity for growth and personal development.

He guessed he had grown during the past four years—grown more tolerant, more settled—more cynical?

Landon saw Diana coming across the lobby of the Hallivand cafeteria at half-past 12:00 on Monday morning. While he had had some apprehensions about the meeting, he was relieved to see that Diana was wearing magenta, an almost certain sign, he mused, that she was feeling expansive. He could see that she had just had a haircut, the close-cropped natural curls hugging her head like the bathing cap his mother used to wear when they went swimming in Lake Michigan when he was a boy. He smiled at the unsuitable comparison. When his mother was 36, she had worn gray or green plaid cotton housedresses, even to go shopping, and he could hardly remember what she looked like without an apron over the housedress.

"Hello, Landon," Diana said, not pausing when she reached him, but assuming that he would fall into stride with her as she went on toward the central service line.

He followed, almost at her elbow, picking up a tray and a packet containing fork, spoon, and knife.

"Were you able to find a furnished apartment somewhat to your tastes?" she asked, glancing over her shoulder.

"At least something that will do for the time being," he said. "Its location is its chief asset although it is comfortable, and I'm getting settled by pieces."

"I meant to ask you if you wanted some of the house-wares. Kitchen things and bedding. Wedding gifts, etc."

Landon shrugged. "Maybe. A few baking utensils. You probably won't need them." He couldn't remember Diana cooking anything more complicated than steaks and baked potatoes. Mostly they had eaten out, except when he cooked for the boys on Saturdays while she was shopping.

"My lawyer says proceedings should be quite simple since we are mutually agreed about major considerations," Diana said. "Maybe in three to four weeks we can have everything settled and closed." She took her ticket, glanced down the column of figures, and paid the cashier.

When they were seated at the table, Landon decided to bring up the subject of visits with Ryan.

"I know it is hardly customary," he said, "but I feel that allowing me to spend a few hours each week with Ryan would cause you no particular hardship. The boys are quite attached to each other, you realize. Could something be written into the agreement?"

Diana opened her napkin and spread it carefully over her lap. When she looked up, the in-control look had evaporated. She was clearly disturbed, not angry with him for asking, Landon decided, but grieved in some surprising way.

"You've always loved him, haven't you, Landon?" She looked straight down at the elaborate salad on her plate, and Landon noticed the interesting pattern where the whorls of her double crown overlapped in soft silver-gold ripples. He hated her perfection for its falseness.

"While his own father . . . I guess the most important reason I married you was that Ryan was so taken up with you."

He wanted to break her beautiful mask—to shatter her poise.

"And so that I could relieve you of your responsibilities—of all your frustrating hassles with child care. You never wanted him in the first place, did you? Why didn't you have an abortion, Diana, instead of bringing Ryan into the kind of world you live in—a card to play or discard as the mood strikes you?"

As soon as he said it, he realized that he had gone too far. He could not afford to make an enemy of her.

Should he apologize? No, he decided, he wouldn't. He gave his attention to cutting his meat, then chewed meditatively, glancing covertly at Diana. The muscles around her lips tightened, her hands set tense on either side of her plate, her eyes fixed on a piece of asparagus.

"We agreed," she said, "to work out the details between us considering the fact that divorce lawyers make a living complicating matters so that they can charge higher fees. I am reiterating, Landon, so that we do not become distracted by peripheral issues."

"Excuse me," he said. "I'll try to be more tactful. However, Ryan is not a peripheral issue." He paused but did not want to give Diana time to speak before he had finished. "From my point of view, he is a central issue. For his happiness as well as my own, I would like to establish some agreement by which I may spend a designated period of time with him, say weekly, or at least twice a month. Is that reasonable, Diana?"

She looked at him, evasively, he felt.

"Is it?"

"Why isn't it?"

"I suppose . . ."

"The rest is so simple," Landon said. "You own your car. I own mine. Insurance, retirement, you name it. Everything has been kept separate from the beginning. No common property."

"Neither is Ryan common property. Let me remind you of that."

Landon swallowed. He would not become angry. He had decided that.

"Except that for four years you have been satisfied for me to take the role of a father, doing the parenting when you were too involved in—whatever . . ." He couldn't trust his voice. "I'll call my lawyer," he said. "He's a very creative person. He might think of something."

Neither of them finished the meal. Landon left the table after 10 minutes in which neither of them spoke. He took the elevator to the mezzanine and went out on the rooftop garden. A sprinkler moved in swift short spurts across a raised bed of pink flowers, leaving a semi-circle of wet paving. It was hot—blistering. He remembered how in the dream all that concrete and steel towering on the left came down on him. He shuddered, walked around the terrace twice, then went back into the upper lobby and on up to his office.

In-company mail had been delivered while he was out. New directives concerning use of Hallivand's air service. An opportunity "to provide even finer protection for the wife and children in the event of your untimely death." A letter from the head of engineering. Well.

He scanned the sheet, picking out the salient points. Possible promotion. Excellent record of service. Recent contributions to financial stability of the company. Enhancement of company's public image. Private interview tomorrow. If it works out, to meet with directors Thursday. Well.

He hadn't sensed that his work had received that much attention. Landon wondered if department politics were involved. Probably. He placed the letter inside the locked compartment over his florescent light then smashed the envelope end-wise in his hand and threw it with some force into the trash can. He felt panic, bitter in his mouth. *Out*! he thought. *I want out*. But that was impossible.

He had been with Hallivand since he turned 20, had started on a work-study program the university was running at that time. For 15 years he had been climbing—

slowly some of his associates had remarked. His immediate supervisor had been the one who mentioned the slowness, warned him of his lack of competitive spirit.

If I am promoted, Landon thought, *I'll be two levels above him. Just like that.* In spite of the locked-step procedures built into the "career ladder" of company policy.

Politics.

Yet after 15 years' experience. With my record of solutions to complex problems. Mixed, of course, with a number of significant failures.

Mike Reynolds, head of engineering, opened his office door.

"Harris! Good! I have some very tempting ideas to propose to you. Come in."

Landon did not sit down in the chair Reynolds indicated since Reynolds himself remained standing, opening several portfolios, removing drawings, shuffling the materials as if he were deciding on a rhetorical approach for a major presentation.

Three hours later when Landon left his office, he had agreed to meet with the directors and very likely accept the position especially created for him, a position in which he would have unbelievable freedom to put his skills to the stretch, a position in which his abstract reasoning could have full play, but in which he would also be allowed hands-on, on-site applications in creating prototypes.

"We appreciate solid work," Reynolds had said. "And we recognize solid work when we see it. Remember that."

At his apartment Landon opened a can of beans and thrust a piece of bread into the toaster. It was only half-past 6:00, but he was exhausted.

Landon fell asleep on the sofa with the television on but the sound turned low. His dreams shifted and swayed like images in water or the special effects sometimes used in the movies to give a dreamlike impression. He kept turning up in the neighborhood of his childhood with aging houses made into apartments, really quite respectable, all of them with a patch of lawn front and back with flower boxes under the windows. He saw his mother, the window sash thrown up, leaning out, tending her geraniums, red ones, pouring water from a plastic pitcher, yellow. The water pouring into the box and dripping down.

Dripping down. He was on the sidewalk below, looking up, maybe a boy of 10. No, 8. The water dripped to make a tiny pool in a dent in the sidewalk just in front of his tennis shoe. The water pooled in the dream up to his knees, and he was in the park with all the neighborhood kids, his parents on a blanket in the shade of the elms beyond the fence. He was chasing his sister Mary who had the green plastic raft they shared. Only she kept it just out of his reach. The water slowed him down, but she leaped out of the water, jumped ahead of him in an astonishing way. He fell face first into the water, his eyes open, and glided forward like a boat with the motor turned off but moving ahead . . . His mother drying him in a towel afterward.

But in the water again. Lake Michigan again. His mother was in the water with them, nearly to her waist, wearing her navy blue swimsuit with its loose skirt that floated out around her and made her look wonderfully fat as he lay on her hands in the water learning how to swim. She was wearing that rubber swim cap that was sculptured to look like damp hair hugging the head. When she leaned over, he threw his arms around her neck and pulled his face against the cool wetness of her neck.

Then she took up his brother Tom. His father was there. He was on his father's back, his legs circling his waist, his arms gripping his shoulder, and together they went out into the waves, the mild waves swelling all the way to his father's chin before they stopped to look far out at the blueness, the cleanness of the sky and the water. Waves rose over his shoulders and over his father's hairy shoulders. The water was cold, but his father was wonderfully warm where their bodies met. Dreaming, he was bathed lavishly in a sea of security, a security gone when he awoke—dead—as dead as his parents who slept in the Cedar Lawn Cemetery.

When Landon awoke, a sit-com was going off, followed by its final commercial. He turned over. His arm had gone to sleep.

The apartment was dark except for the patch of light where the draperies were not completely closed and the rainbow light from the television screen spread across the carpet, up the wall to the ceiling.

He lay on his back, thinking about his father, his mother. They had died together in a car accident on the freeway six years ago. That seemed to him to be the turning point. Everything had been different for him since they died. As if he had sealed off his emotions into an inner chamber in which no one else could enter. That was the time, he reflected, when he began closing Joetta out. When had he seen Mary last? Or Tom? Cards last Christmas. Tom was an industrial worker, making a good living. Had a nice home in the suburbs, three kids. Mary was a nurse. More like his mother than he would have imagined she could ever be. Three kids and working a night shift. He'd never seen the youngest. Hardly recognized her husband in the picture on the card—so much heavier than the stringbean he was when they married just out of high school. Still lived in the old neighborhood in a housing project that had replaced some of the row houses. Happy? He guessed so. Had never heard otherwise.

How long has it been since I was happy? Landon thought. He couldn't remember when it was. Moments of pleasure. Yes. Times when he felt a certain pride or satisfaction. Yes. He had been proud of the Feltwhite Project, pleased at the recognition that went with that success.

22

Proud of Diana's advancement, pleased because she seemed more relaxed with her new job in public relations. Proud of the boys. Yes. Yes.

But mostly the past five—six years had been like the Indian legend with the bear struggling to climb the stump, digging in his claws and pulling himself up while the stump grew taller faster than he could climb. Was that Devil's Tower? somewhere in Wyoming. He hadn't so much as filled a flower pot, and yet he always seemed to feel the dirt under his fingernails where he had been trying to get a grip.

He held his hands up, looked past them at the shadow they cast on the wall behind the sofa, remembered making shadow men or animals or monsters on the walls like this for Robbie and Ryan when they were smaller. They had made up stories and created regular dramas. It was a game they played when he put them to bed on Saturday nights before he and Diana went out. The boys would settle down, giggling and making up more stories when he turned out the desklamp they used making shadows.

"Night, Dad," they would say together, Ryan's voice velvety soft, and Robbie's pitched a little higher.

"Don't you miss Diana?" Peggy had asked last week.

"Not really," he had said.

But he did in some ways. Not in the usual sense of missing someone. A more negative missing. He had so much time on his hands now, and that wasn't bad. And the silence. That was good. And the tender moments. Even the most tender times had been marred after the first few weeks they were married. After the euphoria of having what he had set out to get. Diana had been a prize. For someone successful. Someone smart and going up. Well, he won that prize. But the contest didn't end with the wedding. Diana was still up for the highest bidder. So to speak. Not in a cheap physical way. Diana was hardly intimate enough, even with a husband, to be . . . She was just going up, always going up with the elevator with whoever pushed the right buttons. Not that she needed a free ride. She was tough. Brainy. Power hungry. Whatever her own brains and persistence won was never enough, didn't take her fast enough. It was as if she had climbed onto his shoulders then sprang away from him, reaching for somebody else a little higher up the ladder.

"The trouble is," Peggy had told him, "you keep looking for a meaningful relationship. For Diana, any relationship has only one meaning—her own upward mobility. You're a sucker, Landon. You don't need Diana."

Meaning, of course, that she would be glad to provide solace, reinforce his ego.

If he didn't need Diana, he certainly didn't need Peggy. Why were women always just like their mothers?

Peggy's mother had married Diana's father less than three months after his wife died of cancer. With her it was the money. Anderson Melton offered little in the way of social status, just the money that could buy a little more notice with some people. Diana wasn't cheap. Anderson was. Just a shoddy wheeler-dealer who managed to make enough money to become a big time entrepreneur.

Landon sat up and pounded the pillow, leaned back on it, then pounded it again. A side glance at the television showed the weather map with the man flashing his pointer around like a magician's wand, as if he were creating the storms that he said threatened the Mid-West on Friday.

Maybe a thundershower would cool things off a little, Landon thought. Who cared what kind of weather the weekend brought? Robbie would be in Waterford with Joetta and her parents, and Ryan would be watching cartoons while the housekeeper read the want-ads.

He wondered how Joetta's father was doing. Robbie had seemed worried. Ellison Smith must be past 60 now. Heart attack. The second. His wife was off on sick leave, spending most of the time at the hospital.

"Grandma sleeps at her house when we're there," Robbie

24

had said. "Mom makes her. Mom sleeps on the little fold-down bed in Granddaddy's hospital room."

He had described the fold-down bed with the same attention to detail he used in describing his grandfather's bathrobe and the rails he had to climb over to get into the bed to stretch beside him and listen to his heart beating.

"He's going to be all right," Robbie said. "I heard his heart with my ear right over the sound. Granddaddy told me it was still a pretty good heart."

Robbie was the Smiths' only grandchild. They didn't actually spoil him. And it wasn't as if they were reliving the times when their son was a child. They understood Robbie, maybe because age and distance had made it easier for them to fathom childhood. Their son had been a disappointment. But how could a son who just lit out for somewhere, with never a word then or later, be a disappointment? They had no way of knowing how he had turned out after the first wild flight of late teen years. Maybe he had done something to make them proud of him, only they just didn't know about it.

They're disappointed because they've lost him, Landon thought. *No matter how successful or fine he turns out, if they don't know, if they don't have him . . .*

Just like I'm losing Ryan.

The meeting with the directors was little more than a matter of form. Landon could see that they had come to a decision and that their questions were designed more to reassure him than to confirm their own judgment of him.

"Are you willing to step into this position?" the chairman asked him when they had finished.

Landon Harris thought of the fish in his aquarium the summer he finished graduate school, the summer just before he left Joetta, when she was working 50 hours a week, when he had so little time between studying and caring for Robbie that he gave up keeping up the apartment. A green scum had developed on top of the water. He had felt like those fish, their mouths breaking the surfaces, making a sucking sound as the bubbles of their breathing burst and tiny droplets of spray in the glow of the florescent lights. Desperation for some breath. Since then there had been mostly green scum, stagnant hopes and dead memories bubbling up in a gaspacho gone sour.

He left the conference room, walking to his office, down the wide passageways then down increasingly narrow ones between hundreds of cubicles made by connecting the hundreds of portable panels covered with pearl gray fabric of specially insulated material, both dense and lightweight so that the entire complex could be reorganized in whatever ways seemed most efficient according to the long term work plans of Hallivand Steel—he felt as if the city itself had miniaturized, with each passage the remnant of a street, each block of cubicles an apartment complex, etc., etc. And inside the cubicles, men like himself, or women, closed in from seeing who worked on the other side of the partition, but hearing, in spite of the high-density materials, that person breathe or cough or sigh, the voice on the telephone, the printer spewing out information important in some way to that other person in his work—knowing that person, male or female, sat in a chair like his that glided on soundless rollers across the carpet from keyboard to file, that person reached for the standard reference works on a shelf over the florescent light—a florescent light glowing into the small aquarium, like his own, where the other person gasped for air, or at least a glimpse of the sky or a summer tanager springing the twig of the blackjack oak outside a window. A window. Any window. How could this be called vision where there was no vision?

What else was there to do? Landon felt the algae-filled water thick around his face. If a person kept climbing, was there air on top? Did a man ever get above that green slimy stuff? So he had a major promotion!

Saturday the thundershower predicted for Friday hit. More than a shower, it began with rumbles and cloudy skies before dawn with rain sheeting straight down by 9:00. Out of boredom Landon decided on visiting a Jewish synagogue. It might be clearing on Sunday. Who could tell? He was glad his apartment complex provided covered parking. And an attendant at the Jewish center parked for him. Real convenience.

He was unfamiliar with the music or even the Scriptures, but he enjoyed the ritual. He stayed after services for the social hour with coffee and rolls and friendly conversation. When he left, the sky was still heavy, but the rain had stopped.

Landon drove to the mall, planning to take in a show, buy a new tie, maybe pick up a magazine. He ended up spending the entire afternoon in a bookstore browsing through bestsellers—nonfiction—everything. He bought a cookbook, a book about aircraft for each of the boys, and a Bible.

Inspired by the cookbook, he stopped by a supermarket. At home he made spinach lasagna, dividing the recipe into four portions, three of which he froze in the foil trays he had saved from frozen dinners. After eating far more than he should have, he sat down at the table with the Bible, which was a rather plain one. He hadn't realized how expensive Bibles ran.

This one was the same translation that he had read in a college literature course, so filled with memorable passages, with a nice sound when he tried a psalm aloud. Musical. Strong. All right.

Before going to bed, he put the two books for the boys in envelopes and addressed them. He would mail them on Monday.

Maybe it was the quieting effect of the Bible the evening before, but Landon awoke early Sunday morning, relieved that the rain had ended. He called a man from engineering and made a date for tennis and lunch then sat down with the Sunday paper in front of the television. Funny how after telling the boys to keep the thing low, he felt strange in the apartment alone without another voice, even a distant one thrown at him by that thing. The program he left on was made up very much like the newspaper with features and conversation and news bits. He divided his attention between the program and the newspaper, extracting nothing in depth from either one. He read the funnies, and when he was done, a preacher had taken over the television, the same soft-spoken man with a Bible open in his hands of the "Babylon is fallen" sermon, reading and talking.

I should turn this off, Landon thought.

Instead he got his new Bible from the kitchen table and turned to Revelation 14, the chapter which seemed to be the center of discussion.

"Wouldn't you like to be one of this group?" the preacher asked. "Wouldn't you like to be a part of the victorious number singing about their victory?" Landon was scanning the verses the preacher had mentioned.

"And in their mouths was found no guile," the preacher read. Landon mouthed the word. "Guile," he muttered again. He liked that word. It had a snaky sound to it.

"Are you tired of deceit and complicity? Tired of make-believe relationships in a world constructed of flimsy word pictures? Do you want your life to be totally transparent, clear as fresh rainwater?" The preacher closed his Bible and looked straight into the camera so that it seemed to Landon he was looking at him eye to eye.

"Are you sickened by guile? Jesus Christ can give you both the role model you need and the power you need to live above the manipulative, controlling, world of selfishness in which you find yourself."

Landon switched the television off and dressed for the tennis match. Even on the court as he flew from one maneuver to the next, trying to outguess his opponent, feigning, sweating, he thought about that word. *Guile*.

Trying to go to sleep that night, staring at the bedroom ceiling, he thought of the people he had encountered in the churches he had visited—all of them searching for light through the stained-glass windows or in the flawless rhetoric of the pastor, the thousands of faces all turned toward the face glowing under the spotlight behind the pulpit. All in the flawlessly tailored suits, men and women with scarves and ties reflecting the stained glass colors, all glowing in the dark. Were they all of them, like him, gasping for air?

The following Thursday Diana called.

"I don't know what you and your lawyer have come up with," she said. "But I talked to mine, and he saw no reason why we can't arrange for Ryan to spend alternate weekends with you—the weekends you have Robbie, the boys' friendship being the compelling reason to maintain the connection. This is, of course, not a permanent or binding agreement but on a trial basis. Is this the weekend Robbie spends with you, or does Joetta have him?"

"I'll pick Ryan up at the library at 6:00," Landon told her. He suspected guile. He accepted the package. For now. At least the guile wasn't out of his mouth.

He had seen her twice during the previous week with a senior vice president. *Busy social life*, he thought. *Convenient to have Ryan occupied so he doesn't interfere with the good times*.

Well.

Landon spent the better part of Thursday and Friday being briefed about his shift from his current position to the new one. Of course, he had to tie off the projects in which he was involved, or at least bring them to such a state that the man filling his place could proceed without confusion or duplication of effort.

"I believe I'll need most of a month to be ready," he told

Mike Reynolds, the head of engineering.

"Too long," Reynolds said. "Three weeks at the most. This is the time to move ahead. Aggressive action, you know."

Landon had heard that line before, too. "Whatever success I have is the result of my own work style," he said. "I am neither ambitious nor aggressive. I am curious. I am methodical. Possibly imaginative."

Reynolds smiled. "I suppose we can afford to be indulgent of your feelings," he said. "But three weeks, not four."

"And another thing," Landon said. "The office on sixth is fine. But no secretary, please. If I need clerical help, I'll call for someone through temporary services."

He had visions of a carbon copy of Peggy showing up in the reception area in his new complex, complete with immaculate desktop, carefully modulated voice on the telephone, a voice scattering far and abroad any information to which she had access.

Saturday he took the boys to an air show. Sunday they visited another church.

"The Catholics had a better organ," Robbie commented as they drove back to the apartment, "but I like the Presbyterians' singing better."

"Why?" Ryan asked. He hadn't been to the Catholic church with them.

"I don't know," Robbie puzzled. "I know some of the songs, I guess."

Ryan tapped Landon's shoulder. "Does his mother take him to church?"

Landon glanced at his son. "Does she, Robbie?"

"No. But Grandma used to sometimes."

"I wish I had a grandma," Ryan said. "Does yours make cookies? I read about a grandma who made cookies. In the picture in the book they didn't look like Oreos or anything like that. The kids in the story liked to watch their grandma bake cookies."

Landon listened with one ear to the discussion about the value of grandmothers while he worked through traffic to a place the boys liked to eat on Sundays. Entertainment in the form of kids' movies and video games and huge animal puppets that engaged the children in conversations while they filled up on hot dogs or pizza.

While the boys ate and dashed occasionally from their table to follow the shambling bear, Landon sat guard over the catsup and half-finished French fries and the bottled soft drinks. He sat thinking about grandparents. Ryan couldn't remember Diana's mother really, for she had been hospitalized for nearly a year before her death, and while she had been attached to her grandson, she was hardly a warm person. A little more class than Anderson Melton. A little more integrity. Landon had often thought that if it hadn't been for her mother, Diana probably would have had an abortion. There had been some talk of putting Ryan up for adoption, she admitted once, because she was still in college. But then . . .

His own parents had doted on all their grandchildren. Holidays Mary and Tom and their kids overran their apartment, running up and down the stairs until the old lady below banged the ceiling with her broom handle, objecting to the noise. Robbie was toddling then, not quite 2 at the time of the accident.

"These kids are my contract with immortality," his father had said once, Tom's oldest on his lap, and Mary's leaning against his knee.

And Joetta had said . . .

Landon couldn't remember just how she had put it.

"Don't you plan on living in heaven, Dad?" Landon thought that must have been what she asked because his father had grinned and shrugged.

"Never have had much confidence in political promises," he said. "Now, a fine bunch of grandchildren like this. They make it worthwhile for a man to put in an honest lifetime of

31

work. If I can leave each of them with a little college fund and some solid human values, I figure that's about all the reward I should ask for. Anything more is pretty much speculation."

Robbie couldn't remember them. But then, he had Joetta's parents.

Landon thought about growing up with four grandparents and seven great-grandparents, all living within the same section of the city. That was rich even if they didn't each have a savings account designated for his college education. Well.

The divorce was listed as no fault; as a result there was to be no trial, only a brief hearing with the judge before they signed the papers.

"No fault," Landon muttered, entering the justice building by one of the side entrances.

Maybe neither he nor Diana was really to blame for the breakup. It had been inevitable, and he had sensed that almost from the beginning. Where the fault lay then, was in their marriage itself, which should never have occurred. He had been a fool to run like a greyhound in the races after a fake rabbit. An utter fool. It had been flattering to have Diana notice him at department staff meetings and then to have her single him out in the cafeteria, to have her pay such attention to his small successes. He had been so vulnerable then. Such a fool!

And he had felt frazzled. Worn out from night classes, finally taking a semester's leave of absence to finish graduate school. But Diana knew he was moving up and kept telling him so. Pushing him? Yes, even before they were much involved, or before he sensed it, at least. She had filed for a divorce from Rogers first, seeming to prove to him that she was serious about their relationship, committed. And he had asked Joetta—told Joetta he wanted out.

He had offered to pay her $20,000 for the years she had

worked to keep him in school. She had laughed at him.

"Do you think I want your money? Like a loan cleared with the bank. A financial contract, all obligations fulfilled?"

But she hadn't used Robbie as a pawn. They had agreed that however they felt about each other, they wouldn't hurt Robbie.

The judge reviewed the agreement.

"Mr. Harris," he said. "Do I understand that you are requesting joint custody of a stepchild, Mrs. Harris's son from a previous marriage?"

"That is correct, your honor." Landon glanced at his lawyer, but there was no sign of encouragement.

"Highly irregular," the judge said. "You had not legally adopted the child, I assume?"

"No, your honor."

"Then by what rationale do you establish any claim?"

Landon tried to explain the relationship between Ryan and Robbie and his own love for the child. After a few moments, the judge raised his hand for silence.

"Mr. Harris, our first consideration is always the welfare of the child. It seems to me that if in situations like this, when the adults in the case have a history of unstable relationships, it is better for the child to be as free as possible from the complicating factors. While your interest in this child may be sincere, and while you may feel a profound sense of loss in being separated from him, I feel that it would be damaging in the long term for you to seek to maintain ties with him. Therefore, I deny your request for joint custody and suggest to his mother that she also deny any prolonged relationship between you and her son. I realize that it might be necessary for the boy's sake to let him become used to the changed family situation over a period of weeks, but I recommend that the sooner the break is made, the sooner the healing process can begin."

33

After the hearing Landon's lawyer took him by the arm. "You can appeal, of course."

"No," Landon said. "I don't believe in fighting over children."

In a few weeks Diana would be married to *whoever*. What if Rogers had stayed in the picture or even Ryan's natural father Peter Andrews? Ryan's life was already complicated enough.

He called Diana that evening, but she was out, the housekeeper told him. He called her at work the next morning.

"Do you want to explain everything to Ryan," he asked, "or will you give me a chance to bind things off myself? I promise I won't make you out the bad guy."

"I've already explained the divorce to Ryan, and I believe he understands," Diana said.

"I just don't want him to feel abandoned," Landon said. "I want him to know he isn't to blame in any way."

"Oh, isn't he?" Diana asked, her voice suddenly sweet— sickeningly sweet. "How do you suppose a woman feels when the man she marries prefers spending every evening with a small child?"

"He's your child," Landon reminded her.

"Yes, you've told me that before."

"So, do I get a chance to tell him goodbye?"

"Do you want him for the entire weekend?" Diana's voice had taken on the bargaining tone she used when arbitrating in-company disputes. "Because, if you are willing to take him for the entire weekend . . ."

Landon was becoming exasperated. "Does this mean that you do or do not mean to follow the judge's advice?"

"I haven't yet decided," Diana said. "A great deal depends upon what Klein and I decide. We haven't discussed the matter."

Landon stared at the bare wall opposite his desk. "I don't want him this weekend. Nor until I have a concrete understanding of what arrangements will be made for the long term." He hung up.

"Granddaddy is getting better," Robbie told him the first thing on Friday. "Mom's going up to help Grandma bring him home from the hospital tomorrow. And next week I can go up and see him at home."

"That's great!" Landon said, truly glad that Joetta's father had made it.

That evening after supper Robbie unpacked his duffle bag in the bedroom while Landon cleaned up the kitchen. Robbie came back before Landon was finished and perched on the stool opposite the sink. He placed a book on the counter.

"See what Grandma got me."

It was a Bible story book like the one Robbie had read in the doctor's office a few weeks past, Landon noticed.

"I took one of those little cards," Robbie said. "Grandma mailed it in. She's getting me the whole set."

"That's great!" Landon said. "Let me open my mail first. Then we'll read some of your book."

Robbie sat down on the floor in front of the sofa, leaning against his shins, turning the pages of the new book and tentatively reading the titles. Landon shuffled through the junk mail, setting the few pieces of real mail to one side. H'mmm. A letter from a steel company in Pittsburgh. He didn't remember subcontracting any work with them. He tore the envelope apart and scanned the letter. If he understood it correctly, this was a job offer, or at least the offer of a job offer. He went back to the beginning, reading carefully. As he read, he realized that there had been an information leak somewhere. Someone in Hallivand Steel had advance notice of this offer and had prompted the promotion, seeing that everything happened with dispatch. It wasn't so much that Hallivand wanted to give him room to grow. They didn't want him to move to Pittsburgh, taking all he knew about their systems and plans with him.

Still, the Pittsburgh firm knew his record, recognized a valuable engineer when they saw him. Or maybe they were into piracy. More green scum. He needed air.

"Are you ready to start reading, Dad?" Robbie asked.

Landon folded the letter and placed it in his shirt pocket. "Yes, let's read," he said.

Robbie opened to the title page and read, "*The Bible Story,* Volume One." There was a picture of children peering into a blue jay's nest. Robbie turned two more pages. There was a picture of a father, Adam, presumably, and two boys, all clad in skins, leading a calf, or trying to. In the background was a woman, presumably Eve, for she was dressed in skins as well.

How can they all look so happy so soon after being evicted from Paradise? Landon wondered.

"I've already read most of the first story, but you can read it again," Robbie said.

Saturday they drove up the Michigan shore, stopping at public beaches every few miles, buying fruit from a roadside stand and a loaf of bread, a package of sliced cheese, and a bottle of cold lemonade from a quick market at a service station.

"My parents used to bring us up here on Saturday afternoons when I was your age," Landon told Robbie. "My sister Mary, my brother Tom, and me."

He found the state park had changed considerably, even the beach.

"This is where I learned to swim," he said.

They got out their swim suits and went down to the water. It wasn't as clean as it had been then. The sand along the water's edge was littered with cigarette filtertips with wisps of white paper and shreds of tobacco. Cans and gum wrappers and disposable diapers. They walked along the shore, talking, deciding not to swim after all. Landon tried to describe the feeling he had when he learned the water would hold him up without his parents' arms under him.

"My swimming teacher didn't do it that way," Robbie said. He took Landon's hand and looked up at him. "But I know what you mean. Mom and I went to the lake at Waterford once last year. It's different from in a pool."

That night back in the apartment when Robbie was asleep in the other single bed, Landon lay awake. "We haven't hurt you, Robbie," he whispered. "Your mother and I." He wondered if Ryan had spent the entire day watching television while the housekeeper fretted about not having the weekend off.

The best thing about his promotion, Landon decided, was that he had a spacious office to himself and that office had a window with a broad view of Hallivand's green sloping grounds and the row of lombardies that blocked out the freeway. This Tuesday morning he stood, the narrow decorator blinds pulled completely back, looking into the rich greenness of the hillside trying to absorb some restfulness. A robin wheeled down from one of the tall poplars in a spiral that ended in the grass where the bird was only a dot but still visible since Landon had watched his descent and saw him land. At the far edge of grass a grounds worker wrestled with a riding mower, the significance of his struggles lost at this distance. Landon turned to his desk where the work he had begun yesterday lay in two and three thicknesses of computer printouts, wide sheets like ribbon draping onto the floor on either side. He reviewed his work and cleared his desk, then accessed the program and began playing with his math to see what would happen if slight changes were made in his equations.

This was the best part about his work. He could play with things, seek startling innovations, brilliantly simple solutions. And he had time. While he worked he could block out his private world and the power structure of Hallivand

Steel. In the silence of his new office, he felt the possibility, yes, it *was* a possibility of rest.

As yet he had made no reply to the company in Pittsburgh. The offer fluttered in the back of his mind like a moth on the outside of a window screen at night. He felt annoyed.

At 10:00 he was interrupted by a call from Reynolds. An unexpected team meeting for the Breakcliff Project. And what did that mean?

A little discussion about the technical problems and a whole lot of guile. How had he managed to define life before he discovered that word?

Landon thought of the years he had spent reading thousands of screenfuls of data, printing it, reading it in hard copy, revising, comparing, shredding it all and forcing it into plastic bags, securing it with plastic twist strips. Guarding the files. Protecting the information. Only there was no light, only data, information—very bright people and very bright machines, all glowing in the darkness of Hallivand's soaring complex.

At the meeting Reynolds' assistant singled him out, as if to keep him occupied with several sets of formulas while the three other team members talked with Reynolds around the planning table. Did he imagine they discussed something they wanted to keep from him?

Landon was hardly back in his office when Joetta called.

"Daddy's had another heart attack," she said, her voice thin, frightened. "A massive one. I'm leaving immediately. Robbie's at Teresa's. He'll need to know right away. He'll want to go. But I'll lose at least an hour if I pick him up."

Landon glanced at the clock. "I'll take a long lunch break and run over there. Is that what you want me to do?"

"Yes. And can you figure out what else to do for him. I'm too upset to think."

"I'll call the hospital to let you know what we work out," Landon said.

"Whatever happens . . ."

After Joetta hung up, he sat there still holding the phone. It was as if somewhere inside himself, somewhere just outside the reach of conscious articulation, something swelled almost like a child's cry for help. It was nearly 11:00. He called Reynolds.

"Don't worry," Reynolds said. "You haven't called in sick since I've known you. Take however many days you need to be with your boy."

Landon decided to run by his apartment first, pack a suitcase for himself and another for Robbie, and then swing by Teresa's. He had better call Teresa first so she could feed Robbie his lunch and have him ready to go.

"But don't tell him about his Granddaddy," he said. "I want to be with him."

He called the Waterford hospital and left a message for Joetta.

They were headed northeast out of Chicago on the Toll Road. Robbie, his seat belt secured, seemed smaller than his usual self, huddled, fearful.

"Dad, he has a pretty good old heart. He said so, and I heard it. It sounded like a good old heart."

Landon looked at the boy. He nodded. "But even good machines wear out, son. It might just be that your Granddaddy's heart is worn out. You've seen pictures of the heart and understand how it's a pump that keeps on working day and night as long as a person lives—never gets any rest. It's bound to wear out sometime."

Robbie nodded, his head down.

"I've been praying," Robbie said.

"Good," Landon said.

He remembered losing his grandparents, one after another until he was a married man. Then he realized with

39

a shock that his father's mother was still living. What have I done? he thought. When I married Diana, it was as if I buried everything from my former life, as if no one, nothing from before existed. Nothing except Robbie.

He wondered if Grandma Harris still lived with her sister Mabel in Groveland Manor. If she still wore pink gingham dresses and a white hair net over her snow white beauty shop curls. Landon looked at the speedometer. He settled his foot a little heavier on the accelerator, switching lanes and moving ahead of an 18-wheeler.

"We'll be in Waterford in a half hour," he said. "Do you know where the hospital is located?"

"Real close to the freeway so it's good for the ambulances," Robbie said. "There's a big H on the exit sign and an H beside the stoplight."

Joetta was with her mother outside the cardiac unit when they arrived. She hugged Robbie and spoke briefly with Landon. Since Elliot Smith was not conscious, and since he was currently receiving emergency treatment, Robbie could not see him.

"There's a small park about a block from the front entrance," Mrs. Smith said. "That would be a better place for you and Robbie to wait than here."

"If he wakes up . . . " Robbie began.

Joetta hugged him again. "If he wakes up, I'll come for you right away."

It had been a year since Landon had seen Joetta. He was surprised that she was so thin. So tired. But, of course, she had been under a lot of strain.

He checked into a motel down the street and changed his clothes. He bought a newspaper and picked up some of Robbie's books from the boy's duffle bag. They walked back to the park. It was nearly dusk when they walked to the hospital, bought some chips at the snack bar, and went to the cardiac unit's waiting room.

Mrs. Smith sat with her face in her hands. Joetta came to the door to meet them. She shook her head. Landon took her arm, and the three of them went to the sofa.

"Is Granddaddy dead?" Robbie asked.

"No," Joetta said. "But he's not going to wake up, Robbie. He's going to die very soon. That's why Grandma is crying."

Robbie pressed his face into the front of his mother's dress, his small shoulders trembling as he hugged her fiercely. Landon looked away, embarrassed that he was helpless to comfort either of them. Embarrassed at his own pain.

Elliot Smith died almost two hours later. Landon stayed on in the motel, keeping Robbie with him until the funeral since Joetta had no one else to look after him while she made funeral arrangements and cared for her mother.

The funeral was held Thursday morning in the small Presbyterian church that the Smiths attended. Burial was in the cemetery beside the church. Although Landon sat with Joetta and Robbie, he felt as if he sat at the bar of judgment before these people who had been Elliot Smith's lifetime friends and neighbors. He left immediately after the services, tense. He knew he had done the right thing in coming and in staying by, but he was angry with himself.

Without knowing why, he drove on to Detroit, spent the night in a very expensive hotel, got drunk for the first time in his life, then the next morning drove south without any plans—just driving, moving because he could not be still, compelled by the way he felt about himself to try to out-distance himself or lose himself switching lanes and taking unexpected exits in the traffic.

Monday morning he was back at work, still keeping himself company in his own skin, trying now to bury himself in computer files. The whole week he expected interruptions, but none occurred. Each day was filled with his work on the Breakcliff Project. No calls from either

Diana or her lawyer. No further communication from Pittsburgh even though he had written a letter declining the job offer. He closed everything out, concentrating on ideas that had been teasing for attention for several days, and finally the solution which he expected became clear. Landon began filing in folders all the printout materials that showed the steps by which he had achieved the finished calculations. He drew plans, wrote proposals, defined objectives. He knew when he submitted his work to Reynolds before leaving Friday at noon that the project was ready to fly as soon as committees approved it.

For two more weeks he spent his working hours flushing up possibilities for the next project, talking with the directors, wandering around engineering listening to the current frustrations of men he had been working with for years, scanning data files accumulated in the OPEN drawer of his system. This time might have been unsettling, but it wasn't. If he didn't slow down, he couldn't think too much.

At home he opened cans, sometimes not even bothering to warm what was in them. He read a lot, and watched television a little. He thought about calling Grandma Harris but didn't. It would be awkward explaining four years of total neglect.

On the second Sunday he picked up the same preacher on television. The one with the sermon about *guile*. He was still in Revelation, moving rather slowly, to Landon's mind. Landon got out the Bible and found chapter 18.

"Babylon the great is fallen," the preacher read, "and is become the habitation of devils, and the hold of every foul spirit, and a cage of every unclean and hateful bird."

Landon listened as he went on to read of the sins common in Babylon and the plagues that would fall upon that city. Landon realized that because he had missed several sermons, he lacked the foundation on which to base an understanding of this discussion. But when the preacher closed by reading the challenge, "Come out of her, my people," he felt frightened. Bound for judgment. Condemned. He turned the television off and sat for a long time contemplating the closed drapes, his eyes running up and down the folds of the fabric, trying to see. But there was no light.

Landon was cooling off after a game of tennis, enjoying the air conditioning and his iced tea, watching the three couples in the pool moving languidly in the water. He thought about showering and swimming for a while himself, but he was too comfortable just then to move.

"Mind if I join you," a voice broke in.

Landon turned. A blond man, maybe five years younger than himself, stood with a drink in one hand and a tennis racket in the other.

"Sit down," Landon said.

After talking generalities for a half hour, Landon stood up.

"It was pleasant getting acquainted," he said. "My name is Landon Harris. Let's get set up for a tennis match soon."

The other man seemed thrown off balance. "I'm Kevin Rogers," he said.

"Oh," Landon said.

After an awkward silence, he sat down again. "Then we have a lot more in common than playing tennis," he said. "I don't know if you were aware that Diana and I just completed a divorce." He paused, rubbing the condensation from the outside of his glass with his pointer finger. "And let me apologize for my unbecoming behavior four years ago."

Rogers raised his eyebrows. "From appearances, you did me a favor, even though I didn't recognize the fact at the time."

"About the only damage done is to my pride," Landon said. "It hasn't been all that great a marriage for either of us. A mistake from the start."

Rogers seemed embarrassed. "How's the kid? What's his name?" He bit his lip. "Diana didn't have him with us when

43

we were together," he said. "I saw him a couple of times at her mother's. But usually when we were there, he was somewhere with his nanny. We weren't a very domestic pair, you know."

"Ryan's doing fine. Eight years old now. Enrolled in a primary school for gifted children," Landon said. "A great kid. After meeting you, I'd kind of like to meet Ryan's father. I think he'd like a chance to give the boy a little security now that I'm out of the picture. Did you ever meet Peter Andrews?"

"No," Rogers said. He hesitated. "But Peter Andrews is not Ryan's father. It's anybody's guess who is. I was already involved with Diana and her crowd in college when the kid was born, and Andrews had been out of the picture for a long time by then."

"Then . . ."

"I'm not the kid's father, if that's what you were going to ask me."

"I wish I were," Landon said, getting up. He stood for some time staring at the empty chair. "I would still like to arrange a tennis game with you some time."

For the remainder of the day, Landon tried to think of how this information affected his relationship with Ryan. It seemed to him that if no one had ever come forward as the boys' father, then . . . Then what? *Guile?* Blackmail? Making Ryan a hostage in a court battle?

No.

"I used to be a rather decent guy," Landon told himself as he unlocked his apartment door that evening. "Just not very smart."

So where did he go from here? After Diana he was in no frame of mind to become interested in a woman, even on a casual, friendly basis. He could remember, not too long ago, when he would have taken some terrible risks to have the income he had now—or the job.

In the middle of August Peggy called his office.

"I'd like to see you, Landon," she said. "Could we have lunch together?"

Landon waited for her to explain her mission, but she said no more, obviously waiting for him to speak.

"Not today," Landon said. He had no other appointments, but he wanted Peggy to know he was anything but eager.

"Tomorrow then? At 11:30. I'll take an hour and a half so we can go somewhere more private than the company dining room."

"Sorry. It will have to be here," Landon said. He had no intention of driving Peggy anywhere for lunch, let alone to participate in a cozy tête-à-tête in some exclusive little restaurant.

"Really?" Peggy asked. "Are you tied up that tight?"

"I'm afraid so," Landon said.

The following day he took the elevator down to third, and he and Peggy went on down to the atrium together, both of them uncomfortable, he thought.

"What has come up that you needed to see me?" he asked when they had begun eating.

Peggy smiled cautiously, a dimple showing before she spoke.

"Diana asked me to sound you out before she speaks to her lawyer. She's putting Ryan up for adoption."

Landon found he was unable to swallow the food in his mouth.

"She thought you might like advance notice in case you were interested in adopting him yourself. Of course, a couple with a stable marriage might be more desirable, but . . ."

"Tell Diana to have her lawyer contact mine," Landon said. He took a quick drink of water to ward off the choking sensation he felt.

"Does that mean that you are interested in adopting Ryan?"

"That's correct," Landon said.

"I told her you would be," Peggy said. "Anderson was against the whole thing at first—wanted to move Ryan back to his house and hire someone to take care of the boy, but Mother convinced him that such a situation would be totally unworkable. Can you imagine Mother managing a small boy?" Peggy laughed.

"No," Landon said. "I cannot imagine."

His mind raced through dozens of possibilities, booby traps that might be lying in his path. Could Anderson Melton prevent the adoption if Diana arranged it? If she once signed papers, could she change her mind and take Ryan back? Would the court allow a divorced man to adopt a child? He would have to hire a housekeeper. Could he find someone young enough to be helpful, intelligent enough to be a fit caregiver for a boy like Ryan, and plain enough to make a scandal out of the question?

"I told Diana that Ryan needed a mother more than he needed a father, but she was bound to give you first chance. She said she thought you'd made him a very good mother." Peggy laughed again. "But then, you will doubtless marry again before too long . . ." her voice trailed off suggestively.

"I don't anticipate such a move," Landon said. "If you'll excuse me." He rose. "Tell Diana, as I said, to contact my lawyer."

"You needn't rush off," Peggy said. She smiled.

"Yes, I must," Landon said.

Peggy was as unsafe an ally as she was an opponent. Right now he was not sure how she should be classified and couldn't trust himself to respond appropriately. Not that he thought Peggy had enough influence with Diana to sway her once she had made up her mind, but it didn't hurt to play things safe.

He went directly to his office and called his lawyer.

"I don't know what to make of it," he admitted. "Except that an 8-year-old son is a liability in the marriage market or possibly in her career." He thought of mentioning his conversation with Kevin Rogers but didn't.

"Don't seem too eager," the lawyer advised. "Let me handle this."

"Just don't take any chances of losing Ryan," Landon said. "I cannot emphasize enough how important it is both to the boy and to me that I be able to adopt him legally."

He heard the lawyer draw a satisfied breath. "Consider the boy your son," he said.

After hanging up Landon wondered if he should make any other calls, perhaps call Diana. Not yet, he decided.

He wondered what she had told Ryan, if anything. Maybe she was leaving the explanations to him.

How do you explain to a boy of 8 that his mother finds him a pain? he wondered. How do you tell him that she'd rather do the social scene, build a dazzling career? Would he have to explain? As perceptive as he was, Ryan already knew all that.

Landon stood for a half hour looking out the window where the sprinklers flung water in overlapping circles across grass struggling against the August heat to keep its green.

He wanted to call Teresa's and talk to Robbie, but of course, it would not be sensible to tell Robbie about the adoption until it was certain. Robbie had experienced about all the pain he could handle for this summer.

I'll need a larger apartment, he thought. *I'll have to ask the boys whether they want to share a room or have rooms of their own.*

Fortunately the work spread on his desk did not demand total attention. He sat down to consider the safety features of a building design worked out by veterans in the engineering department, checked the specifications in the manual against those they had written, looked for exceptional features which might throw off the calculations.

Diana called him at his apartment about 9:00 that night.

"You win," she said. "I've never been a mother to Ryan, only played at it occasionally. And to tell the truth, I don't like the role. Since I'm to be married over the Labor Day weekend, I'd like to work out the preliminaries before then so that you can take custody by the end of August."

"And what if you change your mind after Ryan moves in with me?"

"I won't," Diana said. "You'll have to trust me that far, Landon. I believe my lawyer said I would have 90 days in which to reconsider after I sign. But keeping Ryan with me and making him fit into my new marriage for such a short time seems totally unnecessary and foolish."

"Just when do you want me to come for him?" Landon glanced at the calendar. He had Robbie this weekend and again over Labor Day.

"I've packed all his toys and clothing," Diana said. "Could you come tonight?"

Landon bristled with caution. "Yes," he said finally. "I'll be there in a half hour."

"Hi, Dad," Ryan said when he opened the door.

Landon could see from the looks of the apartment that Diana had packed not only Ryan's belongings but most of her own as well.

"Klein and I are buying a restored town house," she said. "The movers are coming tomorrow."

So that was it! She was moving in with her upwardly mobile man. Only he didn't want all her baggage. *It would feel good*, he thought, *to be a little violent*. Instead he assessed the number of boxes next to the door.

When Landon realized that he would not be able to get

all of Ryan's things in his car, he called a cab. It was nearly midnight by the time they had all the boxes and suitcases inside his apartment. He had still not had a chance to talk to Ryan alone, and now it was so late that the child was too tired to talk. They located Ryan's pajamas and toothbrush. The rest of the unpacking would have to wait.

"You won't mind sleeping in Robbie's bed tonight?" Landon asked.

Ryan grinned and shook his head.

"Robbie will be here Friday," Landon said as he turned out the light. "Since there is no space for another bed, I'll have to sleep on the sofa when he comes."

Ryan sighed, almost a comforted sigh, Landon thought.

"Good night, Dad," he said.

Landon shuddered in the other bed. What if Diana didn't make it with Klein—whoever? What if she demanded her son back? No, he decided. Had she ever wanted Ryan? She was glad to be rid of him. Glad to be rid of both of them. No sweat. He turned over, his body still tense. What if Andrews showed up sometime in the future? Say in a couple of years. And then he remembered what Rogers had told him in the country club. No, Andrews was out of the picture entirely. Landon stretched out on his back, his arms folded in a pillow under his head, his body finally submitting to the realization that he had little reason to expect complications in the adoption proceedings.

Before Ryan was awake the following morning, Landon called Teresa and explained the situation.

"Ryan has never stayed with a sitter before except at home," he said. "But on such short notice I can hardly find an acceptable day care facility. Could you manage at least for the remainder of the week?"

Robbie was still at Teresa's when Landon came by for Ryan at 5:15.

"Really, Dad, is it so?" Robbie asked, his eyes bright.

"I hope so," Landon said, gripping his son's shoulder.

The boys hugged each other at the door and winked as if they had talked everything over and now shared a new secret.

"See you tomorrow," Robbie said.

Driving back to the apartment, Landon searched for a suitable way to begin the conversation with Ryan. They were turning into the parking area when Ryan spoke.

"Dad?"

"Yes, Ryan."

"Dad, I'm glad."

"So am I," Landon said.

"I knew you would be," Ryan said, pressing the button to release his seat belt. "Mom said she was at her wits end what to do with me. I don't know why she didn't think of letting me live with you. She saw how sensible it was right away when I told her that's what I wanted."

"Your mother is a sensible woman," Landon said.

"Yes, she's smart, all right," Ryan said. He sighed as they locked the car. He came around and took Landon's hand. He looked up.

"As long as you want me . . . " he began.

"I want you," Landon said, grabbing the boy in a bear hug.

There was closet space for Ryan's hanging clothes, but Landon moved most of his own things out of a dresser into cardboard boxes and put Ryan's things in the drawers.

"We'll look for another apartment on Saturday when we're all together," he said.

"How many bedrooms?" Landon asked, looking up from the Apartments for Rent section of the paper on Saturday morning.

"If you legally adopt me," Ryan said, "we won't be

50

stepbrothers anymore. We'll be real brothers."

"That's right," Landon said.

"Then if we're real brothers, shouldn't we have a room together?" Robbie asked.

"If you want to," Landon agreed. "But some real blood brothers kind of get in each other's hair when they share a room. They get along better with a little more space of their own."

Robbie and Ryan looked at each other.

"I don't need that much space," Robbie said. "What good is a brother if you can't be together with him?"

They made a lot of calls and looked at 10 apartments that day, but in the end they settled on a larger apartment available in the same complex in which Landon lived. And since the other apartment was empty and already prepared for the next occupant, they arranged to move immediately. A man from maintenance came with a large cart to help them, and by transferring packaged things to the floor and using the same boxes to pack the next load, they had everything moved by noon on Sunday.

Landon looked at the situation in the kitchen.

"Let's go out to eat," he said.

They were in the middle of dessert when Robbie laid down his spoon. "Dad, we didn't go to church," he said.

"No, we didn't," Landon said.

"I went with Grandma last Sunday," Robbie said. "She said it made her feel a lot better."

"I'm sure it did," Landon agreed.

Ryan looked at both of them, surprised.

"We've been tasting churches all summer," Robbie explained. "Some have better flavors than others, but we rather like them all."

Robbie took up his spoon again and drove it deep into his Boston cream pie. He took a big bite then licked the chocolate syrup off the back of his spoon.

"Do you choose a church by its flavor?" Ryan asked.

"Not really," Landon said. "But because we weren't just sure how a person does go about choosing a church, we started checking for flavor. Before we settle on any particular church we'll have to find out the correct criteria for judging churches."

"Grandma says it's all in the Bible," Robbie said.

Landon wiped his lips then looked at the chocolate on his paper napkin. He was as weak on chocolate as the boys were.

"Yes," he said. "I'm sure it is all in the Bible."

"The rest of my Bible story books came," Robbie said. "I could leave half of them at Mom's and half of them with you. That way Ryan can have some of them to be reading."

Ryan seemed a bit puzzled about the turn toward religion, Landon thought as he settled in the bed in the master bedroom. The boys had left their door open, and he could hear their voices like the soft sound of crickets in short bursts of conversation, slowing now as they became drowsy. Tonight they had read in the Bible story book, and for once Robbie was in territory in which he had superior knowledge.

"Did all of this really happen?" Ryan had asked when Landon closed the book.

While Landon hesitated, Robbie answered.

"Of course. If God said it happened, it happened. A person doesn't argue with God, you know."

"I guess not," Ryan had said.

"Good night, Dad," the boys said.

In his own room, Landon looked at the ceiling. He felt like addressing God in a personal way, like asking some of those questions himself. He had never actually prayed in his life although he had listened to quite a few prayers on public occasions, and, of course, he had read some of the great prayers in literature. But nothing personal. He remembered the opening words of the Lord's Prayer.

"Our Father which art in heaven," he began.

He got no farther. He was suddenly overcome with the significance of those few words, as if when he uttered them he acknowledged a binding relationship.

He was aware at once of the love God must feel for him and the deep commitment to take care of him. He acknowledged that behind all the tangle of his personal affairs, God's hand had been in control, opening situations, closing others, providing solutions where none seemed possible.

That's the way Dad used to do for me when I was a kid, he thought.

He remembered times when his father had disciplined him, sometimes quite severely by modern standards.

Strange, he thought, *that I never thought he was mad at me or didn't understand. Strange how much I trusted him.*

But then, his father had never broken trust. He made mistakes, and he admitted that he did. But he never broke a promise, and he never told a lie.

At least as far as I knew, Landon thought.

He wondered if his father had ever been sidetracked by any of the problems he had messed up on. Probably not. He lived in a different world where it was pretty hard for a man to have any respect from the community, let alone self-respect, if he left his wife and kids. And as far as ambition was concerned, a man with less than a high school education couldn't realistically hope to move out of the lower ranks in industry.

Landon was still thinking about his father, coming home from work, smelling of sweat and coal dust, sitting down on the stair to take off his steel-toed boots while the three of his children sat one above him, one beside him, and one below—Landon was still thinking about his father as sleep stole in.

"Our Father which art in heaven," he whispered, consciously praying for the first time in his life.

PART TWO

MONDAY Landon received a large packet of Ryan's documents from Diana through in-company mail service. Everything from birth certificate to immunization records and, of course, his report cards from first and second grades and achievement test score printouts. Landon called the number listed for the school for gifted children to confirm that Ryan was registered. They told him that Landon would have to come in to fill out additional forms because of the change in family structure.

The adoption, it turned out, would require considerably more time than Diana had intimated or he had expected, but within a few days Landon received legal guardianship.

"That's the first hurdle jumped," his lawyer told him.

Landon discovered that in June Ryan had been enrolled in a summer recreational program which included both recreational and educational activities. So at least until school began, he wasn't pressed to find a housekeeper.

"Do we have to have one?" Landon asked Ryan one evening later that week. "I mean, I can cook and do laundry. You could probably learn how to make your own bed."

Ryan leaned against the cabinet, watching as Landon rolled crust to spread over the vegetable-cheese pie. Ryan smoothed some of the flour with the palm of his hand, then with his pointer finger drew a smiling face.

"I could hire someone to clean everything spic and span once a week," Landon said, folding the crust in half and laying it across the top of the pie. He began crimping the edges.

"But what about when you go out?" Ryan asked. "I'd be scared."

"I may not go out much," Landon said. He slashed two air vents in the top crust and set the pie in the oven.

"What about parties and receptions and all that? You and Mom went to a lot of parties with your friends. Almost every night sometimes."

"Do I have to?"

Both of them burst out laughing.

Ryan searched his face. "Don't you like to, Dad?"

Landon washed his hands. "Not much. I've endured enough parties so far to keep me satisfied for several years."

"Robbie says his mother has never had a housekeeper," Ryan said. "She doesn't like parties either. And Robbie helps her with the housework. He cleans the bathroom and vacuums."

Landon put his hand on Ryan's shoulder. "Good for Robbie."

He sat down with his evening paper while Ryan turned on a ball game on television. As he scanned the paper, he considered how much more sane his life would likely become.

In the four years he was married to Diana, he had become accustomed to a social life that made the most of the money they were earning, the status they were acquiring, their business contacts. He had joined a health club and a golf club and a service organization which the company encouraged employees above a certain level to belong to.

Diana had an ever-changing, ever-expanding circle of friends who gave "fabulous" parties, and, of course, they expected to be invited to Diana's parties. Diana usually threw her parties at her father's country place, occasionally at the club.

It's surprising, Landon thought, *how people always go to such pains to make their parties unique and how most parties turn out to be very much the same.* Almost everyone, as far as he could see, went to parties more to avoid strong personal friendships than to build them. Often he thought of parties more as just another climbing tool than as entertainment—a very serious one too. He wondered how much of his success at Hallivand was the result of social contacts—strings pulled by Diana's friends. Diana's business was pulling strings. How good an engineer was he really? Well, without Diana he would find out. Maybe she had dumped him because she recognized he had gone about as far as he could. He winced, the muscles in his middle constricting in that now familiar knot.

He looked at Ryan, the child's face tense as he watched a slow motion replay of an out on second.

"Who's ahead?" Landon asked.

"Home team," Ryan said.

Landon laid down the business section of the paper and turned to local events.

He saw several announcements of Labor Day celebrations planned by churches or civic groups. He noticed that the neighborhood parade to which his parents had always taken him as a child was listed. He wondered if Mary and her husband took their kids. Mrs. Anderson Melton had had a tea. She was pictured with two other local women and the winners of the women's golf tournament which closed yesterday. Well.

He dropped the paper, leaned back on the sofa, and closed his eyes.

"When will the pie be ready?" Ryan asked. "I'm hungry."

After they ate, Landon looked up Mary's phone number and called her.

"Would you accept a wandering brother if he showed up at your Labor Day picnic?" he asked.

His sister sounded alarmed.

"No, Diana won't be with me. Just the two boys. What shall I bring? A watermelon and a case of soft drinks?"

"I can remember coming here," Robbie exclaimed midmorning on Labor Day when they neared the street of row houses where Mary and her husband lived. "We came here for Christmas once when I was little. I remember a Santa Claus. He let me try on his boots. They had fur around the tops."

"And they were so tall, so big, that you fell down when you tried to walk," Landon said. He remembered too. That was the last year he and Joetta spent Christmas together. Her parents had planned their festivities for Christmas Eve so they could take Robbie to Mary's Christmas Day. For him the day had been a disaster.

"Let's see if you can recognize Aunt Mary's house," Landon suggested.

"They all look so much alike," Robbie said.

"Kind of like apartments only a little more separate," Ryan observed. "Do poor people live here, Dad?"

Landon thought. "Compared to what?" he asked. "They don't make as much money as I do, if money is what you mean, son. But I grew up a few blocks from here in a house almost like these houses. And I didn't feel poor."

"How much money did your father make?" Ryan persisted.

Landon laughed. "Nine thousand a year. Maybe ten. But we weren't poor. I know that because my mother didn't have to work."

"Was that before inflation?" Ryan asked.

"It must have been," Landon said.

Tom and his family had already arrived. He and Mary's

husband were taking out a portable barbecue, and two of the older children were setting up folding tables and chairs in the backyard.

Landon set the ice chest filled with soft drinks in the shade at the end of the porch and went back to the car to help Robbie and Ryan with the watermelon, which they were attempting to carry between them.

He could see that both his sister and sister-in-law felt awkward greeting the boys. The cousins too. But soon one of Tom's boys, a blond kid about 12, invited them to watch him and one of Mary's girls play mumblety-peg.

Landon sat on the steps with Mary, watching.

"They are so much alike," Mary said. "Which one is yours?"

"Both of them," Landon said. He told her about the divorce and the pending adoption.

"So now what do you do?" Mary asked.

"I guess the best I can," Landon said.

Mary was wearing a yellow culotte with a shockingly purple-flowered top and sandals, but in spite of the colors and the style, Landon was struck with how much she looked like their mother, a little thick around the middle, strong, self-assured. He wondered if her children felt about her the way he had felt about his mother. He tried to analyze his memories, but the fading images evaded his mental tools.

Mary scuffed her toe back and forth on the step. "I wonder if Mom and Dad worried as much about us as I worry about my three. Some of the gangs were rather threatening when we were in our teens, but nothing like the situation now with drugs and AIDS and . . ."

"They kept us pretty close to them most of the time," Landon said.

Mary's face clouded. "I work third shift so I can be home whenever the kids are awake. And Bill works first. We don't even see each other in the mornings."

"Robbie stays with a friend of his mother's while she

works," Landon said. "The same type person as his mom. She understands what we want for him. It seemed to be the best solution."

"What about the other boy?"

"Nursery school. Day care. Live-in help."

"I'd rather have my own set of problems," Mary said. "At least I have Bill for moral support."

"By which you mean?"

"Oh, I don't mean anything, Landon," Mary said. "I just mean it's easier to raise a family with two parents working as a team than for one to do everything alone."

Landon flexed his legs, preparing to get up.

"In spite of all the wrong turns I've taken," he said, "both boys seem pretty solid—secure."

"Just wait five years. Nobody feels secure at 13," Mary said. Her voice held the certainty of a prophetic utterance.

The third week in September, Reynolds in engineering called.

"Landon, we're considering a job in Minneapolis—a shopping mall with three main levels—two department stores with five or six levels integrated. I'd like you to come have a look at the drawings and then, if we decide to take the project, fly up to Minnesota for an on-site evaluation of potential structural problems." Together with three other engineers and Reynolds, Landon spent the following three days studying the drawings.

"Depending, of course, on the soil conditions, distance to bedrock, and seasonal scheduling," Landon told Reynolds when they had finished, "I believe Hallivand could probably do it and come out with a good profit."

Reynolds leaned across the table, his hands spread wide supporting him.

"I want you to take your time—two or three weeks if you need to. Talk to local surveyors and geologists, construction experts. Find out as much as you can before coming back. We have until the end of the year to submit our proposals."

As far as the work was concerned, Landon liked the idea. As far as Ryan was concerned, it put him in a real bind. He tried to think of a few options. Of course, he could hire a woman to live in during his absence. But how could he find someone suitable on such short notice? And if he did find someone dependable, she would be a stranger, and Ryan would be upset. And, of course, transportation would be a problem. There was the three-and-a-half-mile drive to and from Ryan's school.

He called a child care agency, hoping they would have something to suggest. They didn't.

"Why can't Ryan stay with Mom and me," Robbie asked when Landon told the boys about his problem. *So simple*, Landon thought. "We can't do that," he said. "Your mother has enough to worry about getting you off to school before she goes to work."

"But I've never been to Robbie's other place," Ryan said.

"Mom wouldn't mind," Robbie said. "She likes boys."

"This is different," Landon said. "We can't ask Robbie's mother to help us with this one. We'll have to figure out something else."

Sunday morning they did not go to church, but Landon spent the morning reading the Bible story book to the boys, all three of them stretched out on the floor, Robbie copying a picture from Volume 3 while they read from Volume 1.

"Hey, I found out why Jews go to synagogue on Saturdays," Ryan said between chapters.

"How come?" Robbie asked, reaching for a blue marker to make the water in his picture.

"There's this Jewish boy in my class at school," Ryan said. "I asked him, but he didn't know why. This book says it's because Saturday is the earth's birthday. So I guess Jews worship that day to show they believe God really did create the world."

"Doesn't anyone else believe that?" Robbie asked. "I do.

Dad, how come we don't go to church on Saturday instead of Sunday?"

Landon closed the book and rolled over on his side.

"Well, Robbie, I have never thought of that before. I guess what Ryan said about creation is a new idea to me."

Ryan turned over on his back, his knees drawn up.

"Most people don't believe that," he said. "At least not just the way it is in the Bible. I've read a lot of science books that tell about how the world began."

"I don't think anyone can do more than guess how it really happened," Landon said. "Some of the things I studied in science classes at the university were about as probable as fairy tales. People have a lot of ideas." He remembered his amusement over one professor's farfetched pedantics.

"Well, it's not hard to see that what the Bible says makes sense," Robbie said. "God ought to know. He was there."

"But God didn't write the Bible," Ryan objected. "People did."

Landon thought for a minute. "It's strange how I know that writing wasn't invented until a long time after the events in the first part of the Bible. Yet, when I read the Bible account, it seems as if God is truly speaking to me."

"Something like music or poetry?" Robbie asked.

"Something like that. But not just the same. When the organ plays or the wind blows—it's—as if . . . And when I read the Bible . . ."

"Uh-huh," Robbie said.

After lunch the boys went to their room to play checkers. Landon settled down in his recliner with his Bible. He began reading the story of creation again, verse by verse, soaking up the meanings. He closed his eyes, imagining the earth as it was then, so fresh, so clean. He remembered looking out one spring morning when he and Joetta spent a weekend in Wisconsin. The window faced east with a cedar tree possibly 50 feet away. Dewdrops hung glistening at the end of every sprig of the cedar and on the bushes under it. As he watched, there was a sudden diamond shower, each drop catching the sunshine as it fell. A moment later another sparkling shower from the other side of the tree, then in quick succession, a series of small, dazzling showers. At first he had leaned against the window, amazed, responding to the beauty. Then he began to look for a cause. As the dewdrops fell, only a few at a time, he searched the branches until he spotted a small gray-brown bird with a band of red across its head. The bird hopped from one limb to another, shaking loose a fresh spray of sparkles, and finally sprang from the cedar to fly off into the woods.

Landon remembered classes in which the history of modern evolution was discussed. It seemed incredible to him that intelligent men could assume that the complexities of the natural world could just *become* without any source of power—matter from the immaterial, energy without a generating force. As unbelievable as this was the philosophy which conceded a First Cause, creating the matter, supplying the energy, then abandoning everything, watching from an infinite distance to see what would happen, hardly even interested in the results.

Was it intuition or faith? *Whatever it is,* Landon thought, *something inside me responds to Someone. Who else could it be but God?* And when he read the Bible, as he had nearly every day for several weeks, Someone spoke to him. Certainly the voice he heard was not the mutterings of some long-dead sachem. In his soul, he knew he heard God's voice, almost as if the leaves of thin paper fluttered with His breath.

He remembered an old title—couldn't place it— song? Movie? Stage play?

"Somebody Up There Likes Me."

I'm not sure whether He likes me or not, Landon

thought. *I know He loves me.*

While Landon started a pizza for supper, the boys showed each other stunts they had learned in physical education classes at school.

"Think I'll call Mom," Robbie said as Landon diced onions.

Directly Robbie was back with Ryan, somersaulting down the hallway.

Landon wondered what the problem had been. With all the laughter, it couldn't have been anything serious, he decided. He checked the pizza, then finished the salad.

"Are you boys hungry?" he called.

Just after 7:00 while Robbie was getting ready to leave, Joetta called.

"Robbie says Ryan needs a place to stay while you go to the Twin Cities," she said. "Robbie would like to have him stay here if you don't mind."

Landon hesitated. "That would be rather inconvenient for you," he said. "Robbie suggested the idea to me earlier. I told him taking one boy to school before going to work was as much as you could handle."

"You underestimate me, Landon," Joetta said.

"Oh, I know you could manage, but it hardly seems that under the circumstances . . ."

"What circumstances? Ryan is Robbie's friend. That's the only circumstance which has any relevance as far as I'm concerned."

"I may be gone two weeks, possibly three."

"Robbie told me that."

"I'll be glad to pay."

"Landon, just let the boy come for Robbie's sake. I don't take pay for . . ."

"I'm sorry," he said.

He hung up.

"Was that Mom?" Robbie asked.

"You shouldn't have asked her," Landon said. "She's so busy."

"Don't worry, Dad. We'll help," Robbie said.

"When the two of you get together you make quite a bit more noise than one boy does alone."

Robbie slung his duffle bag over his shoulder. "Mom knows all about boys," he said. "She doesn't mind a little noise."

He would be leaving Wednesday. He packed his own things and then Ryan's. He called the school to explain that Joetta would be bringing Ryan and picking him up. He gave Ryan extra spending money when he left him at school Wednesday morning.

"Share that with Robbie," he said. "You boys might go somewhere—do something extra you need a little cash for."

Ryan hugged him. "You'll be back for my birthday. Promise?" The child's voice trembled, and Landon felt the small body tremble in his arms.

Landon held him tight.

"It's nearly a month until your birthday. Of course, I'll be back. No way would I miss the party if I had to fly home and back overnight. I'll call you tomorrow evening," Landon promised.

Ryan burrowed his face into Landon's shoulder, then pulled away, suddenly embarrassed and very grownup.

The team of five flew to Minneapolis. The other members, a woman and three men, would complete their investigations within two days and return to Chicago. Landon would probe for the kind of information that never came to the surface without longer observation.

"You have a remarkable gift for sensing potential problems," Reynolds had told him more than once.

I'm cynical, suspicious, Landon thought. *Only sometimes a vulnerable, stupid fool. Of all the people in the world I don't trust, I trust myself the least.*

After he thought that, he realized it was not entirely true. But he did have a propensity to avoid coming to grips with the hard facts about his own weaknesses. Was it evasion? Well.

His hotel was near the University, presumably because he would need to use the library and interview members of the faculty concerning the physical impedimenta. The company provided a car. He created his agenda.

"Wish you boys were here so I could take you fishing today," he told Robbie when he called Saturday morning from a small town upstate. "I drove up into the lake country. You should see the fall colors."

"Are you going out in a canoe?" Robbie asked.

"No, a motor boat," Landon said.

He asked Ryan how he liked staying with Robbie and his mother.

"She doesn't put up with as much monkey business as you do," he said. "But I like her. When she wants us to settle down, she just says so. She doesn't yell."

"I know," Landon said. "I hope you remember to put your dirty clothes in the hamper."

Ryan laughed. "No, I put them in the washer with a half a cup of detergent."

"I'll take a picture of the fish I catch," Landon said.

As it turned out, he caught only middle-sized fish, but he had another fisherman take his picture holding his stringer, and then he gave the man the fish, explaining that in the hotel he had no way to fry them.

Sunday he drove farther north, enjoying the brilliant gold to scarlet displays. Were they maples and oaks? And of course, birches, a clear light yellow against the blue green of spruces. He rented a cabin on a lakeshore and sat long after dark on the boat dock listening to the waves lapping against the pilings before retiring. Hours later, after he had been asleep for quite some time, he awoke, startled but unaware what had roused him. He lay there listening until a bird call echoed, it seemed, from the far end of the lake.

Was it a loon? Probably. He got up, went to the open window, then stepped out on the deck. He leaned on the railing, shivering a little because he had not put on a robe. The loon called repeatedly. Landon thought the bird must cry, then pause and listen for an answer.

I'm like that, he thought. *There aren't any words to it. Just a cry I never quite dare let out. It just keeps echoing inside me.*

He was about to go in when an answer to the loon's solitary question came almost from the boat dock below the cabin. The nearness and the intensity of the mate's response made the skin on Landon's forearms tighten, the hair rise up. She had been there, silent in the water, all this time, invisible in the shadows cast by trees along the shoreline.

The far loon called again, and she responded. Time after time they called, their voices coming together as they swam in the darkness. Landon was cold. He went inside, back to bed, and shivered under the blankets.

He mailed disks with information he had collected back to Reynolds in the middle of the following week. Reynolds called, asking for more details on a couple of issues. Landon called on Tuesday. The plane would pick him up Thursday.

He bought each of the boys a hand-knit Norwegian ski sweater and a pair of Indian moccasins. He bought Joetta a book—an atlas. After he bought it, he wondered how he could explain such a gift. He had no idea what had prompted him. But when he saw it as he browsed through a bookstore, he knew she would like it.

Landon arrived at O'Hare Field about 11:00, but it was well past 2:00 by the time he reached Hallivand. He left his equipment and his files in his office, spent an hour with Reynolds explaining the most salient of his proposals, then called Joetta at her office.

"Let me pick up both the boys," Landon said, "since I'm finished for the day."

"I won't be home until 5:15," Joetta said.

"Let me take the boys out to eat. I'll have Robbie back in time to do his homework. I've missed them so much."

"Yes." He could picture Joetta smiling into the telephone.

He took Robbie and Ryan to the family restaurant with the shambling bears and the cartoons. They laughed a lot and hugged him a lot and were clearly excited that he was back.

At Joetta's he went in with Ryan to get his things. He handed her the book.

"Thanks," he said.

She took the book, puzzled.

"Just thanks," Landon said. "I appreciate what you've done for Ryan."

"I met Robbie's grandmother," Ryan said as they drove back to their apartment.

"Oh?"

"She's nice. Like in storybooks, but not quite. Nicer."

"Some people are like that," Landon said. "Words hardly do them justice."

"We visited her once, and she came here last Saturday and stayed over until Monday morning. I thought widows were supposed to wear black and mourn. I asked her why she wasn't mourning. She said Robbie's grandfather was in heaven and she missed him but she was glad he was there."

"Oh?"

"I could tell she was sad, though. She seemed happy when she was talking to us, but I saw her crying in the living room when I got up to use the bathroom."

Ryan was silent for a minute.

"Dad," he asked, "is Grandmother Melton in heaven?"

Landon turned off the freeway. He was pretty sure she wasn't.

"I don't know," he said.

"Maybe heaven is just a fairy tale anyway," Ryan observed.

"No," Landon said. "I don't know just what it's like or who is there, but wherever God is, that must be heaven. And I have a feeling I'm going there sometime."

"Why?"

"I don't know. It's like a *home* feeling."

"The kind of feeling Robbie's Mom gets when she goes up to Waterford to be with her mother?"

"Like the feeling I used to have when I was your age and I went somewhere. Anticipating being back with my parents."

They were turning into the parking area at their complex.

"I know," Ryan said. "I felt that way last night when you called to say you would be back today."

Reynolds told Landon to take the next week off since it would take the staff at least that long to evaluate the information he had brought back. Since Ryan was in school it was not possible to leave the city; however, he spent some time at the public library, spent some time at the health club, and went shopping. He bought a devotional book that caught his eye.

Although Ryan's birthday came in the middle of the week, Landon had planned for Robbie to join Ryan and several of his friends at an ice cream parlor that specialized in children's parties. Ryan, usually very formal in such situations, giggled and told a whole collection of third-grader jokes, more relaxed than Landon could remember seeing him with a bunch of kids.

"Well, you're 9 years old now," Landon told him when they got home.

"Mom didn't send me anything," Ryan said. "I guess she's glad to get rid of me."

"There might be a card tomorrow," Landon said, planning to make a phone call to be sure there would be.

When he went back to Hallivand after his days off, he found considerable feedback on his work in Minneapolis, some of it extremely negative. Although he had felt his work there had been very thorough, some of the people on the feasibility team evidently disagreed.

Two of the team who had gone with him to Minneapolis at the outset were among the most vociferous, *almost vitriolic*, Landon thought. He reviewed the work they had done together, wondering if he had stepped on their toes. He could think of nothing unless they had been offended by his painstaking reexamination of their findings before submitting them. But then, they had done the same to his work. Check, double check, then check again. This was standard procedure. Why should any professional object to being corrected or having his written work edited?

"I'm sick of this dog-eat-dog atmosphere," Landon told Reynolds after a particularly harrowing conference. "I should have taken that position in Pittsburgh. Sometimes I think that coming up through the ranks in a company is the worst possible way to maintain harmony. All those who have worked with you think they had as much right to promotions as you did. They're probably right. I miss the human feeling we used to have out on the floor the first few years I worked here. A lot of fine people helped me learn the ropes. Would you believe that today one of those very men had blood in his eye?"

Reynolds had let him have his say, listening with his head half turned, looking out the window. Now he turned his back to Landon.

"Harris, more than half of a man's success, especially after he reaches a certain level in the establishment, depends on P.R. leaders have to know how to manipulate people and circumstances."

"No, thank you," Landon said.

"P.R. isn't all bad."

"What you're saying is that I need Diana to steer me

through the sandbars!" Landon felt as if his midsection were filled with explosives.

"Not exactly . . ."

"Can't a person just do an outstanding job, take his promotions, be decent to the other workers and keep a little honesty—integrity?"

Reynolds turned to face him now. "Why didn't you take that Pittsburgh offer?"

"I couldn't go off and leave my boys," Landon said.

Restless, having trouble getting to sleep, Landon turned on his bedside lamp. He stuffed an extra pillow under his shoulders, then reached for the new devotional book lying on his nightstand. He had started a few days before reading from the beginning but found some of the entries focused on issues so different from his own experience that he almost decided he had bought a dud. But now he began leafing through the book, reading an introductory text here, a paragraph there.

In this frame of mind, he thought, *it really doesn't matter whether I can make sense of what this writer says or not.*

"For the mighty man hath stumbled against the mighty, and they are fallen both together."

The text was in bold print at the top of a page. Landon read it again. The reference was Jeremiah 46:12. *Some picture of the corporate struggle for power*, Landon thought.

He knew nothing of this particular prophet, had in fact, read nothing from that book of the Bible before. He skimmed the devotion based upon the text, but closed the book. He got up and went to the living room for his Bible. He read the text again before turning to the beginning of the book. He was compelled, chapter after chapter, to read on, gripped by the way God warned and called and waited for His people to pay attention.

It was nearly 3:00 when he put an envelope from his nightstand into the 32nd chapter of Jeremiah and closed the Bible. He had just finished reading the statement, "But every one shall die for his own iniquity: every man that eateth the sour grape, his teeth shall be set on edge." He had stopped there, considering all the sour grapes he had eaten, plucked from a forbidden vine. And now his teeth were set on edge. He should have expected . . .

But a few verses later he found God's promise:

"After those days, saith the Lord, I will put my law in their inward parts, and write it in their hearts; and will be their God, and they shall be my people. And they shall teach no more every man his neighbour, and every man his brother, saying, Know the Lord; for they shall all know me, from the least of them unto the greatest of them, saith the Lord: for I will forgive their iniquity, and I will remember their sin no more" (Jer. 31:33, 34).

Landon had only the prayers of Jeremiah as models, yet as he knelt beside his recliner to ask God's forgiveness, the words flowed from his heart as naturally as if he were a child again, sobbing, telling his father he was sorry he had left Mary's bike in the driveway where it was smashed by a delivery truck.

The relief he felt after praying was good. He went back to bed and slept soundly until his alarm went off.

He turned over, looked at the dim light showing under the bedroom draperies, and wondered.

"Where do I go from here, God?" he asked.

Back to work. Back to the hurt feelings and the tangle.

In his office two hours later, he spread the drawings, the specifications, all the stuff out on his desk and on a large folding table he had brought in.

"There has got to be a way," he muttered, "to preserve the struggle for excellence without alienating colleagues. How do I do as nearly perfect work as I am able without trying to show up the other fellow?

"How do I do better work than the other fellow without making him feel his work is superficial or stupid?"

Do I flatter? he thought. *Do I manipulate materials so that it looks like my corrections are really restatements of a colleague's work? No.*

Then what? Maybe accept criticism of my work more graciously, listen to the other guy's ideas with a little more interest, accept some of those ideas with real enthusiasm?

He laughed at himself.

"I've been standing here praying, God," he said aloud. "Did you hear?"

He walked to the window and drew the blinds open. The hillside below had become a late October brown. The lombardies edging the freeway were bare except for a few fluttering tattered leaves. He stood watching the traffic streaming by, traffic which had been present all through the summer but not visible through the foliage.

The men and women, the children, in those cars—every one of them, he thought, *is a child of God just as much as I am. And they all have their teeth set on edge for some reason or other. They've all eaten their sour grapes.*

"God, if you are this patient with human failure . . . Give me some patience."

So from here, he guessed, it was back to the conferences. Back to the team meetings, back before the directors. Whatever. Well.

After he finished reading the book of Jeremiah, Landon noticed that the following book, Lamentations, was written by the same author. He found two texts he read over and over:

"But though He cause grief, yet will he have compassion according to the multitude of his mercies. For He doth not afflict willingly nor grieve the children of men" (Lam. 3:32, 33).

"The precious sons of Zion, comparable to fine gold,

how are they esteemed as earthen pitchers, the work of the hands of the potter!" (Lam. 4:2).

It occurred to him then that while he assumed that all his reading and praying was leading him toward being a Christian, he had not yet read anything of the New Testament, anything directly about Christ. Here, he decided, he would be systematic. He would start at the beginning and read his way through Matthew chapter 1, which seemed to be meant to be understood literally with its straightforward genealogy from Abraham to Jesus. Then the simple statement of the angel to Joseph, "Thou shalt call His name JESUS: for He shall save His people from their sins." And the words, "Emmanuel . . . God with us." Then the stories, some of them familiar on a purely cultural level, and the words of Jesus Himself.

"Blessed are the poor in spirit."
"Blessed are the meek."
"Love your enemies, bless them that curse you, do good to them that hate you, and pray for them which despitefully use you" (Matt. 5:3, 5, 44).

There had been a time when he would have scoffed at the biblical accounts of the miracles of Jesus. Now they posed no problem. He had established a personal relationship with God—more precisely, God had established a relationship with him—and he was simply listening now to a voice. God's voice, through whatever writer He had chosen to have record the data. The parables. The trial and crucifixion. The resurrection. The gospel commission. Then he started all over again a few days later with Mark's Gospel. Then Luke's, and finally John's. By the time he finished the Gospels, Landon realized that while God spoke to the individual heart quite directly from the Bible, He gave each writer of Scripture room to be himself. Obviously God provided for individualism.

And what did all this reading have to do with the

practical person-to-person conflicts with which he was dealing at Hallivand? Landon realized that as he read without resistance to what he read, he processed the ideas and internalized them. Like the verse in Jeremiah said, "I will put my law in their inward parts, and write it in their hearts."

Parts of his Minneapolis work were discarded. Parts were rewritten. In fact, it was he who was given the task of rewriting from a revised point of view. And Landon accepted the criticism and the changes, graciously he hoped. Yes, graciously, by the grace of God.

During this period of spiritual awakening, Landon read the Bible stories with the boys. Robbie was, if anything, ahead of him, reading on his own from the books he kept at Joetta's, which were those covering the New Testament. And since her father's illness and death, Joetta had begun attending church regularly, the Presbyterian Church in which she had been brought up.

On a mid-November Saturday afternoon Landon was taking the boys to a curling match to be held in a nearby city park. They had decided to walk since parking would be a problem if they took the car. The boys were a few paces ahead talking.

"It feels good to go to church," Robbie had told Landon months ago.

Now when he told Ryan the same thing, Ryan laughed.

"Like Dad's 'home feeling,'" he said, and then told Robbie about their conversation about heaven.

"But there's hell too," Robbie said. "The preacher talked about hell in church a couple of Sundays ago. He really told them. Some of the people in the church were crying, they were so scared."

"What's hell, Dad," Ryan asked, dropping back and taking Landon's hand. "I thought it was a bad word. Like 'give 'em hell.' You know how some men talk."

Landon was trying to think of a way to explain hell to

Ryan the way he had heard it.

"It's a huge fire somewhere where God roasts bad people when they die," Robbie supplied the answer. He gripped Landon's other hand.

"Oh," Ryan said. He was silent for some time, and Landon, when he glanced at him, saw that he was troubled.

"I thought you said God loves people," Ryan said, his voice accusing. "You said God loves bad people and good people both. Like fathers and mothers love their kids even when they're bad. You wouldn't roast me in a fire if I made you mad." Ryan's face turned hard. "I don't believe either of you know what you're talking about."

"But it's in the Bible, Ryan. It's in the Bible. Isn't it, Dad?" Robbie was just as agitated as his brother. He tugged urgently at Landon's hand.

"I don't know," Landon said. "I haven't read the whole Bible through yet, of course, but I haven't seen a thing about hell fire in the parts I've read."

"We'll find it when we get home," Robbie promised. "It's there."

"Well, if it is, I hate God!" Ryan said in a low voice, as if half afraid to say it, yet determined to.

"Ryan!" Robbie cried in distress.

They went on to the curling match, and the boys shouted for the team they had chosen as their favorite, but before the game was finished, they became restless and asked to go home. It was cold. Landon decided it was just as well that they didn't want to sit any longer in the wind on the bleachers.

At the apartment he fixed them hot cocoa while they took off the long johns they had worn under their jeans.

"Get the Bible, Dad," Robbie said before he accepted his cocoa. "I want you to find what it says about hell fire."

"I don't!" Ryan said. He tuned in to a football game on television.

Landon had no idea where to begin searching for information about hell.

"Maybe the Bible has an index," he said, turning to the end of the book. Concordance. This must be it since it listed words and gave references. He found *hell* with what seemed to be its biblical definition: "Place of the dead." One after another he looked up the texts in the Old Testament. From what he read, the word meant quite literally that, the place of the dead, whether a place where bodies were burned outside the city or whether a grave. The New Testament texts left him more confused. There was one reference inside a parable which was obviously part of the metaphor. In other places he thought it must mean something at least similar to what Robbie was talking about. The last one was in Revelation. Jesus said, "I am he that liveth, and was dead; and, behold, I am alive for evermore, Amen; and have the keys of hell and of death" (Rev. 1:18).

"What does it say, Dad," Robbie asked, impatient.

"I still don't know," Landon admitted. "But not what you expected it to say."

After they had taken Robbie home on Sunday evening, Ryan balanced himself on the footrest of Landon's recliner.

"I wish we wouldn't always have to read about God and talk about God," he said. "I don't like Him."

"Because of what Robbie said about Him roasting sinners?" Landon asked.

"I guess so. Would you expect me and Robbie to like you if you beat up on us all the time and yelled at us and threatened to roast us if we weren't good."

"I'm sure you'd hate me if I did that," Landon said.

"Some moms and dads do those things," Ryan said, climbing up to settle in Landon's lap. "I saw a program on television. This mom burned her little baby with a cigarette because it cried. They put her in jail."

When Ryan was in bed, Landon sat for a while puzzling over the hell fire issue. He couldn't blame Ryan for his attitude. He couldn't believe that the traditional doctrine treated God fairly. If that were so, how could anyone even pretend to love God? No wonder modern man had turned to atheism.

And yet, if social reports were accurate, many children whose parents practiced the most gross types of child abuse still claimed to love those monster parents. *Or maybe*, he thought, *they didn't really love them. Maybe they were just too terrified to admit that they hated them.*

"You love me, God, don't You?" he prayed before going to bed.

Whatever those preachers said, he still believed that He did.

Joetta invited Ryan to have Thanksgiving with her and Robbie at her mother's. Landon went to Tom's alone.

Mary's family had gone to her husband's people, Tom said. One of Tom's sons was with a school friend visiting relatives out of town.

"You're lucky to have this place of your own," Landon told his brother. "So many times I've wished I had started buying something instead of sinking all that money into rent."

"Taxes are high. And insurance and interest rates," Tom said. "And maintenance. When we bought the place, it was just 15 minutes to my job, but when the suburbs swallowed up that small industrial island, the plant moved 20 miles out. To be honest, I bought the place hoping the kids would have better surroundings to grow up in. Now there's about as much crime and drugs here as in the old neighborhood. I'm worried about my kids. That's the truth. I mean, what can you offer them for values—hope for society—with politics the way they are and business what it is?"

"Do you take your kids to church?" Landon asked.

"Church? Church he says," Tom scoffed. "Churches are about as corrupt as politics or big business! Did you hear about Grandma Harris and Aunt Mabel? They invested $10,000 between them in some television preacher. What did they get? A sweet thank you letter with a request for their prayers and more money if they could see their way clear to send it. And the devil soaking up the sun in some Caribbean island with a harem of floozies!"

"I heard about the preacher," Landon said. "I'm sorry Grandma Harris and Aunt Mabel were fleeced."

"They're all made out of the same sleazy cloth," Tom said. "Mom and Dad brought us up to be decent citizens without any church. As far as I'm concerned, we're better off for their doing it that way."

Landon wanted to tell him about what had happened to him, about the comfort of having a Father again, but it didn't seem like the right time.

"Could we go out to see Grandma after we recover a little from the dinner?" he asked.

"Sure," Tom said.

"Mary tells me you're between wives again," Grandma Harris commented when Landon sat down beside her on the sofa in the apartment she shared with Aunt Mabel.

"I guess you could say that," Landon said.

"Now your father knew how to keep at peace with a woman," his grandmother said. "And your grandfather as well. I don't recall a time during the 56 years we lived together that your grandfather didn't kiss me good-bye before going off to work."

Landon laughed. He remembered Grandpa Harris making a ceremony of kissing Grandma good-bye even when he went to the drugstore for the Sunday paper.

"Well, I liked that. I think all women do," Grandma said, resting her hand on Landon's knee.

Landon put his hand over hers. He noticed how thin the skin was, how fragile the blue veins. He decided not to try to explain about his divorces, either the first or the last.

While he had realized from the beginning that his separation from Joetta was entirely his own choice, he was coming to realize that he had not given Diana much reason for happiness either.

Landon had expected to feel at least some pain if he should encounter Diana and her new husband, Klein. However, when he walked into a pre-Christmas party at Hallivand and found them already circulating, arm in arm, it was as if so great a distance now separated them that what Diana did and with whom did not touch him. Klein seemed relaxed, moving with Diana among her friends, greeting some as if he knew them already, accepting introductions to others as if eager to know them better.

Landon found an engineer he had worked with on a successful project the year before and engaged her in conversation. He questioned her about her work since then, and she asked him about the Minneapolis job.

"After all the changes, I expect it to go through," Landon said.

"You win some. You lose some," she said.

"Landon!" Diana spoke from directly behind him. He turned.

"Klein," Diana said, slipping her arm around her husband, "I want you to meet Landon Harris, my former husband."

"How do you do," Klein said, extending his hand.

Landon shook hands.

Diana smiled. "How's Ryan?"

"Fine," Landon said. "He had an excellent report from school at midterm. He hasn't had a cold so far since cold weather set in."

"You don't mind if we send him a gift for Christmas?" Klein said.

"Not at all."

Landon held his breath as they walked away. He was

surprised. The anger was gone now as well as the hurt pride. Well.

Since Ryan objected to reading Robbie's Bible stories, Landon took him to the public library children's room for a fresh supply of books. Most of the books Ryan chose were about spacecraft and computers. When Landon suggested a storybook, he shrugged.

"That's not true," he said. "It's no fun to read about things that are make-believe."

At home Ryan read his spacecraft books while Landon read the Bible. He was in Acts now, having read of Christ's return to heaven and the deacon Stephen being stoned by the religious leaders. He was impressed with how God brought the zealot Saul through experiences which led him to recognize he had been working directly against God by persecuting the followers of Christ. How Saul had become the Apostle Paul.

Here nearly all the names were familiar, for throughout the city churches, hospitals, and schools bore names of these apostles and saints. Still nothing about hellfire— nothing that shed any light. When he read the story of Ananias and Sapphira, he was shocked that here God had indeed knocked a man and his wife dead instantly when they sinned. Yet, he had to admit that since they had lied in hopes of winning approval for a gift while they actually pocketed most of the money, they deserved what they got.

He was reminded of the television preacher who made off with Grandma Harris's $10,000. He guessed there had always been frauds in religion as in everything else.

In Romans he saw that he had left the narrative part of the New Testament behind and was into deep material. In chapter two:

"Or despisest thou the riches of his goodness and forbearance and longsuffering; not knowing that the goodness of God leadeth thee to repentance?" (Rom. 2:4).

Not terror of punishment but an eventual response to mercy, Landon thought.

"For not the hearers of the law are just before God, but the doers of the law shall be justified" (Rom. 2:13).

How does that fit with the verse in the next chapter?

"Therefore by the deeds of the law there shall no flesh be justified in his sight: by the law is the knowledge of sin (Rom. 3:20).

Landon was confused, reading the next few chapters, by the many references to *law*. He looked for the Ten Commandments in the Old Testament but couldn't remember where they were located. He remembered seeing a picture of the tables of stone with the commandments inscribed on them in one of Robbie's books. He found them, read them, and then read the stories concerning the law.

"I almost need a primer," he admitted to himself.

But if he was confused about some of the elements of the book of Romans, he finished it with a firm conviction that while God expected him to compare his life to the pattern laid down in the law and to seek to live by those principles, it was the death of Jesus and nothing else which assured him of redemption from sin.

Both boys were practicing parts for Christmas programs at school, rather insipid pieces about candy and stockings, in Landon's opinion, when the news the angels brought about Christ's birth was what was really worth shouting about. Of course, Robbie went to a public school where religion must be excluded in order to show no preference for any particular faith. And Ryan went to a private school, which Landon was beginning to see as dedicated to the purpose of making gifted children feel a self-confidence that left no room for God. He wanted something better for them.

"I'm in a Sunday school program too," Robbie told Landon. "Just one of the angels in the choir. I don't get to say a piece."

"The singing is what matters," Landon said.

Landon felt a bit awkward at Robbie's school program, for Joetta and her mother were there, and Ryan wanted to sit with them.

"I want to thank you again for your kindness when my husband died," Mrs. Smith told him.

Joetta looked a great deal like her mother, who at somewhere near 60 had a youthful springiness in the way she moved. Both women were small with blue-gray eyes that always paid attention, mouths that showed a firmness of opinion, yet both eyes and mouths tending to smiles. He watched Mrs. Smith and Joetta as they talked to each other and to Ryan and later as they listened to the program. He kept remembering.

He had married Joetta the summer before his senior year in college. She had worked full time that year so that he could finish, even though that meant postponing her own graduation. It was Joetta who had taught him to be meticulous about details. She had proofread his papers, typed and retyped them so he could turn in flawless work. How many times had she retyped those pages of numerical tables for his master's thesis? She had that look around the mouth then, her face tense as she worked past midnight for nearly a week. That was the spring Robbie was born, Landon remembered. The home stretch for him with only a practicum left. But the next six months had been almost more than either of them could cope with—Robbie had colic every night until he was past 3 months old. Joetta had to go back to work six weeks after the baby's birth in order to keep her insurance valid. His supervisor on the practicum had been . . .

Robbie was on the stage now, ready to participate in an acrostic for which the children held glitter-covered letters and marched around making different words appropriate to the season.

When the program was finished, Joetta spoke to him.

"What arrangements shall we make about the holidays?" she asked.

"What have you and your mother planned?"

She reached back for her handbag, which she had left on the seat behind her. "Nothing yet. We thought the boys might want to be together at your place and at mine. And Mother would like to have both boys at her house for a day or two, if it works out . . ."

"I'd kind of like to make Christmas dinner," Landon said.

Joetta's smile faded. "I was hoping . . ."

"Couldn't we all just have dinner at my place?" Landon said. "I'm a pretty fair cook."

Joetta's smile returned slowly. "So Rob tells me. He gives me a full list of the weekend's menu after he's been with you."

"Oh?"

"I don't mean that I quiz him." She was embarrassed. "He's very proud of your skills."

"Why can't we? I mean, why can't all of us just have dinner together? Your mother needs to be with the kids, and neither you nor I would like to be the odd parent out."

After two more children's programs, the tensions which had marked his meetings with Joetta had relaxed somewhat. And by the time Landon shopped for food for the grand occasion, he was no longer afraid of the Christmas gathering. Ryan, who went with him to the supermarket, wanted to buy the biggest turkey there.

"Just how long do you think it would take us to eat that bird down to the bones?" Landon asked him. "How many weeks can you stand to eat turkey sandwiches and cream of leftover turkey soup?"

Ryan grinned. They picked, as it turned out, the smallest turkey they could find.

"Remember we'll all be together!" Ryan kept reminding him. "Everybody!"

"We'll be five," Landon said. "And we'll want to fix quite a few different things . . ."

"Pie?" Ryan asked. "What kind?"

After rearranging everything in the refrigerator several times, they finally had the food all stowed away.

"Poor Robbie," Ryan said. "He doesn't get to help make the pie."

Although when he bought the complete collection of ornaments for the Christmas tree the saleslady had tried to convince him that the perfectly symmetrical artificial trees, sprayed with colors coordinated to go with specific packages of ornaments was just what he needed, Landon had resisted. He wanted a real tree. He bought it late, and he and Ryan set it up just three days before Christmas so that it would still be fragrant on Christmas Day.

He and Ryan spent a whole evening decking it with sheep made of bits of real lambs' wool, red and gold trumpets, gauzy angels, and blue and white drums.

Christmas Eve, Landon set the turkey out to thaw before fixing a soup-and-sandwiches supper. Ryan was about to turn on the television when Landon stopped him.

"Not tonight, son," he said. "I want to tell you a story."

Ryan perched on the arm of his chair, his head against his shoulder.

"About when you were a boy?"

Landon pulled Ryan onto his lap and hugged him.

"No, about another boy," he said.

He had read the story of the first Christmas in the Bible twice as he worked his way through the Gospels. But it was in reading the parables of Jesus that he came to understand what the Bethlehem story had to do with his own life.

"I'm going to tell you a story about a boy who was lost," Landon said.

"A boy about my age?" Ryan asked, squirming to get more comfortable.

Landon leaned a little farther back until Ryan's head settled on his shoulder.

"No, he was quite a bit older than you. Now, let me tell you."

He began by describing the home of a wealthy ancient landowner with the fine rooms where the family lived and the less beautiful but still comfortable rooms for the servants. He described the good food and the nice clothing. The hard work too.

"Now, this father had two sons," Landon went on. "The older a hardworking boy who felt good about getting the fields planted and harvested, and the younger a fellow who was a good worker too but more interested in having fun than sticking to a job."

"One day the younger son thought about all the money he was supposed to inherit when his father died and began to wish he had some of that money now, for although his father gave him everything he needed, he didn't give him an allowance in cash.

" 'I don't see why I should have to wait until Dad dies to get that money,' he said to himself. It was easy to see that his older brother couldn't inherit the farm as long as Dad was alive. But now, money. There was plenty of money in the bank. So he told his father what he wanted."

Landon paused for a moment. "Now the father could think of several reasons why his son shouldn't take off with that money right now, especially since they had crops in the field and the boy ought to be out there working with his brother. But the father loved his son, so he decided to give him the money and give him a chance to find out about how to manage his own affairs.

"In just a little while the boy was in the big city. He bought a lot of fancy clothes and went to a lot of parties and spent his money very quickly. He had a lot of friends as long as he was buying them expensive gifts and throwing parties where they could have fun. But when his money was all gone, his friends started looking for someone else to have fun with. He sold his fancy clothes to buy food and pay for a room where he could stay. At last he had no more jewelry or clothes to sell. He began looking for work. But jobs were hard to find. The only kind of work he knew much about was farming, so he went job hunting in the countryside. All he could find was a job taking care of pigs. He earned so little that he had poorer food than the pigs got. At last he began thinking about how nice things had been back home with his father and brother."

"He sounds like a skunk," Ryan said.

"Well, I guess he was a skunk," Landon said. "But he set out for home, and let me tell you, when he got home he was even hungrier and dirtier than he had been when he left the pig farm. He wondered if his father might hire him to work in the fields. His father's servants, he remembered, had always had plenty to eat and decent clothes."

"His dad didn't give him a job?" Ryan said.

"I guess you didn't guess any more about this father than the runaway boy did," Landon said. "That dad had been watching down the road every day since his boy left home. On the day when he saw the boy coming, he ran down the road to meet him. He didn't hear a word the boy said about needing a job. He just wrapped him up in his own coat and hurried him into the house."

"Did he punish him?" Ryan asked.

"No, he threw a party. A far bigger party than any the runaway son had had for his city friends."

"I thought this was a Christmas story," Ryan said.

Landon hugged him. "It is," he said. He wondered how he could explain what he meant.

"Ryan, you've seen models of the solar system showing how all the planets move around the sun. And you've seen pictures of the galaxies moving in perfect precision through space."

"Uh-huh."

"And you've wondered if there are people on some of those planets . . ."

"Why not?"

Landon thought of dozens of episodes to science fiction shows they had watched together.

"Well, after God made all that huge universe, the people living here decided they didn't like minding their father and ran away . . ."

"Hey, you're talking about Adam and Eve!"

"So God let them go," Landon said. "He knew they wouldn't believe what He said until they saw for themselves that the world would soon be in a mess without Him. But He loved those people. He couldn't bear to lose them. So he sent Jesus, who was really God's own Son, down from heaven to show men on earth how much God loved them and to bring them back."

"If I ran away, would you come looking for me," Ryan asked.

"What do you think?"

"I think you would."

They sat in the chair together for some time before Ryan moved.

"Sleepy?" Landon asked.

He put the boy to bed then sat up for a long time contemplating God's search for him. For the whole world, Jesus had come to Bethlehem, had grown up to live a beautifully perfect life, and had died to save the human family. But Landon felt at that moment that if everyone else had been faithful to God and if Landon Harris had been the only one on earth who had run away, God the Father would have longed for him and Jesus would have come for him and died for him. Landon had never been one for singing, but when he thought about what Christmas meant to him now, he felt like singing.

The turkey was in the oven, and Landon had already started making piecrust by the time Ryan came from the bedroom. Landon went to the living room door to watch Ryan standing there looking at the tree.

The boy turned and grinned at him. "I know we won't open anything until Robbie and his mother and Grandma Smith get here. I'm just looking."

He drank a glass of juice but wanted to help with the pies before eating his cereal.

Joetta and Robbie and Mrs. Smith arrived before 11:00 when the pies were already out cooling but before the fancy potato dish went into the oven.

Joetta's mother brought a foil-covered bowl to the kitchen. "My cranberry fruit salad," she said. "You don't mind, do you?"

Landon squeezed her hand.

Landon had enjoyed shopping for gifts for the boys, but everything had been gift wrapped in the stores, and he had forgotten the contents of the individual gifts. As a result, each surprise for them was another surprise for him. He sat forward on the ottoman feeling delight over each squeal of joy they uttered.

He knew he had bought them too much—far more than they could appreciate at once, and yet, it had seemed so important to him that this year in particular he must shower them with proofs of his great love for both of them.

Then they discovered that he had not opened even one of the several packages they had piled between his feet.

"Dad, don't you want to see what we got for you?" Robbie said.

Landon read the tags and picked one from each of the boys. He closed his eyes. "Robbie, you pick which one I should open first."

One after another, he opened his gifts as the boys thrust them into his hands. A new can opener. A necktie. A puzzle which had obviously come from a bubblegum machine. A calendar made in Robbie's art class at school. Slippers. A ceramic toad which Ryan had fashioned in his art class.

"Now this one!" Ryan shouted.

Landon noticed that the package had both Ryan and Robbie's names listed as givers. A guide to wilderness camping.

Mrs. Smith laughed. "Now we know what plans these two have made for you."

Suddenly Landon was aware that Joetta and her mother were there too.

It was while they were eating the Christmas dinner that Landon realized why he had invited Joetta and her mother to come. He had thought as he made plans that the boys needed a Christmas with a complete family circle, that the day would somehow be a total failure for Ryan and Robbie if they were separated from each other or if they spent the day without him or Joetta. Now he knew that he had wanted to spend the day with Joetta.

Although she and Mrs. Smith had stayed out of his way while he finished preparing the meal, once the food was ready, they had moved in to set the table.

Now Landon sat savoring the pleasure of such a meal himself. Not since he left Joetta nearly five years ago had he sat at a table set for a family holiday. He thought of the Christmases with Diana, both of them getting up about noon, sick after a Christmas Eve celebration with friends. Ryan would be in the den, the housekeeper hushing him so he wouldn't disturb his parents. And late in the day a picturebook feast with the Anderson Meltons where most of the time everyone was meticulously polite, posing for the photographer. Mr. and Mrs. Landon Harris toasting the hostess, Mrs. Anderson Melton. Mr. and Mrs. Landon Harris with Anderson Melton. Mrs. Harris's son Ryan with gifts. Anderson Melton with his grandson Ryan. And there they would be with their brittle smiles in the society pages.

"I'm going home," Landon had said last Christmas before

the 4:00 dinner was served. He had been too angry to care that Mrs. Melton raised her voice or that Diana's father made threats. He took Ryan and left. The two of them had eaten at a salad bar. Sliced turkey, dressing, and salad bar. All for $7.50 plus tax. Christmas Special. "Don't you suppose I hate it too?" Diana had said.

"Then why can't we just not go?" he asked.

There was no answer.

He had always expected too much. He remembered his own childhood with aunts and uncles, cousins and distant cousins all at his grandparents' homes. Hardly any gifts. But joy! JOY! And he remembered Christmases with Joetta.

Today he had felt comfortable with them all around the table until the full realization came to him. He still loved Joetta. Had never stopped loving her. Now he became ill at ease. He noticed now her reserve, her resistance. Had she thought he designed the occasion to soften her, to win her back? Was she being polite, not for the press, but for the boys?

The meal went on, the turkey, the elegant potato dish, the cranberry fruit salad, the pies. The boys ate with enthusiasm, all the time reminding each other of toys they would play with once the meal was finished. Joetta and Mrs. Smith complimented the food.

Whoever would imagine, he thought, *that a heart so filled with love for those he was with could beat with such a hollow sound?*

After the pie, the women insisted on clearing away.

"I've never eaten a Christmas feast without washing the dishes," Mrs. Smith said.

"And you didn't even have to cook this feast," Robbie said.

Christmases with Joetta. They hadn't been all joy. At first, yes. Promises and dreams. She was working to help him finish the education he needed to move up at Hallivand.

At first he had objected to 50 hours a week, a regular job in a university administrative office, 10 more hours doing specialty typing for a friend who did research papers by the page. It wouldn't be for long, she reminded him. She was investing in their future. Such silly, precious gifts as they bought for each other those first two Christmases. And valentines made of a sheet of typing paper folded in fourths, carefully lettered, pictures drawn with felt markers. In those days he had two pairs of jeans. Two pairs of slacks suitable to wear to work at Hallivand. Then down to one pair. The next Christmas Joetta worked 60 hours during the close of the semester. Bought him a pair of gray flannels with a tweed sportscoat.

"You're going up," she said. "You'll have to dress for your job."

He hadn't had even $10 for a gift for her. The next spring the job with good pay. He began paying off his educational loans.

"I want to keep working so I can pay off my own loans," she insisted.

She liked her job. She had moved up too. Not far, but up.

"Why don't you apply at Hallivand?" Landon asked her.

But she liked the university.

He was living, breathing Hallivand then. That was all right. His superiors liked his work.

Joetta came into the living room, sat down, and watched the boys building something with red interlocking blocks.

"Engineers?" she asked.

"No, Mom," Robbie said. "I'm going to be an architect, remember?"

"I think I might be an astronaut," Ryan said.

He turned and grinned, and Joetta smiled one of her swift smiles. Landon knew she was thinking of something else, only making conversation with the boys.

Landon talked with Mrs. Smith about generalities—the news, politics, glancing often at Joetta and the boys. He felt a fullness in his throat as if his heart had torn loose, had risen, and was beating wildly there. He had caused her so much pain—all of them so much pain. She could never . . .

"Robbie tells me you are going to church quite regularly," Mrs. Smith said. "I'm glad of that."

Landon became aware of what she said only slowly as the words soaked into his consciousness.

"Yes," he said. "I had been going every week, but since Ryan objects so much, we only go the Sundays Robbie is with us." He told her about the hell-fire debate.

"I've often tried to find some explanation of hell fire myself," Mrs. Smith said. "And for the very reason Ryan is worried. I could hardly love a God so fierce as some preachers make him."

"I can see punishment," Landon said. "And destruction of people who ultimately refuse to be saved. It's like radical surgery or amputation. Getting rid of the diseased part of society. I mean, if people do have a freedom of choice, eventually God is going to have to put a stop to it all. But torture? Forever?"

"I've been praying for you, Landon," Mrs. Smith said. "You're a good man, Landon. A good father."

His mind echoed those words for hours.

"But a rotten husband," he muttered to himself after she and Joetta were gone. He would have Robbie and Ryan until the end of the week. Then Joetta would drive them up to Waterford to spend the remaining days of their vacation with Mrs. Smith. He was glad that he had the extra days off from work.

"Too bad it's too cold to go camping," Robbie said as he and Ryan began picking up their gifts and transferring them to their room.

"The first decent spring weather, we'll go camping," Landon promised. "Between now and then I'll have time to study my new book and know how to camp properly. Would you believe it? I've never slept in a tent in my life."

So they found an Army Surplus store.

"We won't buy everything now," Landon warned the boys. "But look around so that we can start planning what we need and how much it will cost to get set up."

Then Friday Joetta came for Ryan and Robbie, and the apartment was silent. Landon's first impulse was to turn on the television. He pressed the ON switch, then while the picture was still coming up, he pushed it again, watching the color fade and the screen turn black. He stretched out on the sofa, thinking.

So where do I go from here, God?

He lay on his back, looking at the late afternoon light fading to gray on the ceiling, an hour or more.

I'm lucky, he thought. *I have Ryan. And I have Robbie part of the time. And none of us are really enemies. The boys seem settled and happy. They're sensible, realistic boys. More realistic than I am.*

So what am I? An idealist. Yearning for everything to be just the way it ought to be. Too late now, Landon. Too late for a pleasant home in the suburbs, a loving wife, two devoted sons, a challenging job, everything comfortable. Everyone happy. Was anyone—anyone ever—happy?

Yes! Yes! I was happy once.

But in life a man couldn't turn off at the next exit and head back to where he had come from. Life was one way all the way. Straight ahead. Yet, his life, the way it was now, was largely the result of his own choices. He could see that.

"Where to next, God?" he prayed. "I've chosen to turn my life over to You. I don't deserve to be happy, but I keep wanting to be. I keep wanting to go back and mend the broken dreams. How? I know what I want. I want Joetta back. I want us to be a family. I want us to start out all over again as Christians. But maybe You can't trust me with that much."

Landon got up and made himself a sandwich. He sat at the table, chewing slowly.

No wonder Diana was so restless, he thought. *She realized all along I still loved Joetta. The irony of it. I blamed Diana for using me for a ladder. While my own ambition . . . No wonder she hated my guts. No wonder she was always jealous, even of the kids. I wanted the connections, the influence, the control—but not her.*

"God, how does a man go about making things like this right? Is there any way? I know You forgive me. But how can they? How can I ever ask them to forgive me?"

Landon put his plate and glass in the dishwasher and wiped the table. He stood looking at the drying formica surface.

Landon's Monday morning at Hallivand began with a committee meeting during which he would make tentative decisions about assignments for the coming year. He was the only engineer there early.

"Have a nice Christmas?" Reynolds asked.

Landon saw he had a new picture of his grandchildren on his desk.

"A very nice Christmas," Landon said. "The boys had a great time."

Reynolds sat down at the head of the conference table and motioned him to another spot.

"I hear you have a rather complicated family situation at present," he said.

"Rather," Landon said.

"Do you think that adopting Diana Melton's son was the sensible thing to do?"

"Of course not." Landon opened his portfolio and began leafing through the half dozen proposals he had reviewed. "Is the right thing ever the sensible thing to do, Reynolds?"

"Probably not."

"It's hard enough to be separated from Robbie."

"Quite frankly, I spend much more time with my grandchildren than I did with my daughter when she was a child," Reynolds said. "It seems shameful to admit it, but it's the truth. I was so intent upon being successful that I hardly—" He thumped both of his hands down on the table. "If I had been more of a father to her, perhaps she would have been better equipped for her own marriage. But you know what I mean, Harris."

"I know."

Two other members of the committee came in then, and the conversation turned to the proposals each had written since the beginning of December. For the remainder of the morning they examined each member's work. While Landon had made suggestions of his own about future directions for product research, his chief function was to evaluate the ideas of other team members and to develop plans for prototypes and finally to test those prototypes for performance under stress. And so, for most of the day he listened carefully.

In something he had read, he came across the idea of reading the Bible through from cover to cover in one year. He decided to try it. So now, with just a few days left before the beginning of the year, he set about finishing the New Testament. He was just beginning the book of Revelation.

It was the book of Revelation which had caught his attention in the beginning. Now as he applied himself to reading all of it, he found that large parts of the book were so deeply symbolic that he had no idea how he was to take them. He was almost certain that some chapters were tied to symbols he had encountered in other parts of the Bible. But how? He kept turning back to the book of Hebrews which he had read only a few days before. One verse he found seemed to help.

"For Christ is not entered into the holy places made with hands, which are figures of the true; but into heaven itself, now to appear in the presence of God for us" (Heb. 9:24).

As he read, Landon pictured Jesus, dressed in white, his eyes glowing like flames, standing in the temple described by John in the presence of the Father. Whatever He was doing there, He was doing it for his people. When he came to the end of chapter three, Landon backed up and reread the final verses.

"Because thou sayest, I am rich, and increased with goods, and have need of nothing; and knowest not that thou art wretched, and miserable, and poor, and blind, and naked" (Rev. 3:17).

He had been that way. He had blamed others when he was guilty himself.

"I counsel thee to buy of me gold tried in the fire, that thou mayest be rich; and white raiment, that thou mayest be clothed, and that the shame of thy nakedness do not appear; and anoint thine eyes with eyesalve, that thou mayest see" (Rev. 3:18).

But the best part followed.

"As many as I love, I rebuke and chasten: be zealous therefore, and repent. Behold, I stand at the door and knock: if any man hear my voice, and open the door, I will come in to him, and will sup with him, and he with me" (Rev. 3:19, 20).

As he read the prophesies of woes and destruction, Landon kept thinking of Jesus interceding, calling, pleading. The world might be about to crumble, its very foundations shaken to pieces, but Jesus stood there between His people and disaster.

I wish I had some help with this part, Landon thought. But he kept on muddling through alone.

Tuesday he had a call from the social worker assigned by the court. She wished to schedule an interview with him and a separate one with Ryan before the end of the child's Christmas vacation.

"Purely routine matter, Mr. Harris," she said. "We need

to know how satisfied you are and how satisfied the boy is before we proceed to the final stages of adoption."

Landon called Mrs. Smith.

"I know Ryan is having the time of his life, and I know he was looking forward to New Year's with you," he apologized, "but I'll have to come for him Thursday evening."

Thursday riding back to Chicago Ryan wanted to know what he would have to do.

"Just tell the lady whatever she asks about," Landon told him.

Friday, two social workers arrived at the apartment. Landon invited the woman into his office while the young man sat down in the den to talk with Ryan.

Landon was prepared for the questions she asked, for his lawyer had briefed him about what to expect.

No, he had no illusions about patching up his marriage with Diana and was not using the boy as a means of maintaining a connection.

No, he had no prospects of remarriage at the moment.

No, he did not need live-in help.

"I suppose you do have some help with housekeeping," the woman said.

"One day a week," Landon said.

Then the young man came to speak with him while the woman talked with Ryan.

"Ryan tells me you're really some cook," he said.

"Want to look in the refrigerator—taste some leftovers?" Landon asked, tense, but a little amused.

They talked about Ryan's relationship with Robbie.

"The boys have thought of themselves as brothers for several years," Landon said. "For most of the time I was married to Diana, Robbie spent weekends with us."

"What concerned me," said the young man, "is that Ryan has now begun to develop a relationship with Robbie's mother and grandmother which might prove to be painful some time in the future. It's almost as if he has adopted them."

"I know," Landon said.

"What, precisely, is your own relationship with your first wife?" the social worker asked, looking studiously at his notebook and writing as he asked.

Landon hesitated.

"I don't know."

"Friendly, hostile, keeping a forced truce?" the young man prompted.

"Almost friendly, I would say." Landon caught himself rubbing his knuckles. "Joetta and I have always maintained peace between us. We were determined from the time of our divorce to give Robbie the right to love and respect both of his parents."

"But it has only been recently that you have begun to do things as a family?"

Landon stood up.

"Don't you think it would have been rather awkward while I was married to Diana to spend family holidays, go to PTA meetings with my former wife?"

The young man looked embarrassed. "Yes, of course." He closed his notebook. "But it seemed to me from my conversation with Ryan that he and Robbie have some idea that you and Robbie's mother might be reconciled."

Landon swallowed. "That would be quite an ideal solution to many problems," he said. "But such a reconciliation is very unlikely. While I have the highest regard for Joetta, we have each built a life independent of the other."

Landon saw the new year in as he finished reading Revelation.

"Blessed are they that do His commandments, that they may have right to the tree of life, and may enter in through the gates into the city" (Rev. 22:14).

The following Tuesday the social worker called his

office. He invited her to come that afternoon to speak with him there.

"Actually, Mr. Harris," she began, "there is little question that Ryan is far more satisfied now than he has been in some time. He seems to suffer from less stress than does the average child in a stable home with two parents."

"I hope that my home is stable," Landon said. "Does a single parent home preclude the possibility of stability?"

The woman leaned back in her chair. "Of course not, Mr. Harris. But given human nature, I mean, a single man is not likely to remain content to spend his leisure with a child."

"You can ask Diana Melton about that," Landon said.

The woman smiled.

"I don't mean to come across as threatening, Mr. Harris. Actually, we are very happy with the way you have handled the transition period. Very happy, indeed. Only a little surprised."

"I had a good father," Landon said. "I've never had to figure out how a father ought to behave."

"Ryan tells me that you have been taking him and Robbie to church."

Landon wondered if Ryan had mentioned how he had objected to all of this lately.

"I hoped that religious orientation might give all of us a stronger foundation than we have had," he said.

"It might," she said. "All in all, you can expect a favorable report from my colleague and from me. You're to be commended, Mr. Harris. You are a very good father."

He had heard that before. At times he thought it was true. At other times he was not certain. Was being a successful husband not one of the conditions of being a good father?

He was thrown off guard the next day by a call from Anderson Melton's lawyer.

"Since Ryan is Mr. Melton's principal heir, it will be

99

necessary for you to confer with him before going ahead with adoption proceedings."

They arranged an appointment for the next week. Landon went home tense. He had feared that everything was going too smoothly in the adoption. He wondered just how Peggy and her mother might be implicated in the whole affair. Or perhaps Melton was scheming to get around their machinations. Well.

It was too early to get up—maybe 4:00, Landon thought, turning on his pillow to look at the digital panel on the radio beside his bed. The numerals glowed, first the date, then the time—1-14—3:57.

In another hour, hour and 15 minutes maybe, he would get up and start the laundry and have another look at the project he had worked on after putting Ryan to bed last night. The feasibility team would meet at 11:00. Again at 2:00. Reynolds wanted the report by 4:00.

Landon turned over, pulling the sheet up over his ear and around his chin. Maybe he could catch a little more sleep. He remembered the call from Melton's lawyer. He pushed that out of his mind, returning to the project report.

The project's specifications played like patterns of light across the blank screen of his mind. He was not thinking, not making any connections. Just formulas. Dimensions. Shapes. In a dream the high-rise was completed, gleaming 60 stories tall. Then a bolt of lightning. And the whole thing sizzled. Meltdown? No, there was dust and debris.

Landon awoke with his heart beating wildly, gasping for breath. He opened his eyes and looked at the familiar lines of light on his bedroom ceiling. Last night he had read the story of the tower of Babel in Genesis. He knew that story had brought on the dream. That and his preoccupation with wind stress factors. He had seen pictures of the remains of ancient Babylonian ziggurats, possibly even the remains of the tower of Babel. Bricks and asphalt blown with desert sand.

Hallivand's steel and concrete . . .

He turned to rest on his stomach.

"My name is Ozimandias, king of kings

"Look on my works, ye mighty, and despair . . ."

That was Shelly. He had memorized that in high school. Pyramids, ziggurats, amphitheaters. Nineveh, Petra, Thebes, Minos, Babylon. Babylon.

Babylon is fallen, is fallen that great city.

Landon got up and showered. It was quarter to five when he finished shaving, eight after when he started the washer with a load of sheets and towels. He fixed himself a cup of coffee and sat down at his desk with the printouts for the project.

Over the holidays he had found the family picture taken when he was 10. He had replaced the paper frame with a bronze one and set it on his desk. He picked it up now.

"The most important thing a mother can do for her children is love their father."

He could remember his mother's voice, the firm inflections, the pontifical authority her voice took on when she made such pronouncements. She had been talking to Joetta. Robbie was a baby. She and Joetta were sitting at the kitchen table. Landon remembered that. Joetta had looked up at him with a smile that burned suddenly, then was gone.

Was that the most important thing his mother had done for him?

Probably.

There his mother stood in the family picture, solid as if she were made of concrete and steel. But he remembered the softness of her breath against his hair when she held him on her lap at the doctor's office. Her cheek against his when he cried after the shot of penicillin.

"Beareth all things, believeth all things,

 Hopeth all things, endureth all things . . ."

Where had he read that? He wanted to add, "forgiveth all

101

things." He didn't suppose that was part of the text, wherever his mind had picked it up. Well.

If Mom and Dad had lived, he thought, *I would never have had the nerve to suggest a divorce.* By implication, he had failed both of the boys in that he had not loved their mothers, either of them, enough. His self-analysis made him sick.

Later that week while Landon was driving Ryan home from a dental appointment, Ryan asked, "Dad, are we still shopping churches?"

Landon realized that recently they had attended the two or three churches nearest their apartment, for no other reason than the convenience.

"I guess we're still open for suggestions," he said. "Why?"

"Oh, the lady who cleaned my teeth invited me to visit her church," Ryan said. "She didn't say she was Jewish, but she said she goes to church Saturdays."

"Want to try her church for flavor?"

Ryan laughed. "I thought flavor was the wrong reason to like a church."

"Well, shall we try it?"

Robbie had been with them the previous weekend. Landon was surprised at Ryan's interest in going to church on the "off" week.

Saturday morning Landon read the address of the Seventh-day Adventist church from the card the dental hygienist had given Ryan. It was some distance from their apartment but near a mall where they often shopped. At least he knew how to get there.

"Let's eat at the mall after services," he told Ryan. "And then shop for some gym shoes for you."

Landon had thought that the time on the card indicated a preaching service. As it turned out, a receptionist whisked

Ryan off to a children's class while a host invited him into the sanctuary where an informal "Sunday school" program was beginning. After a half hour of preliminaries—music, reports, in-group talk stuff—Landon found himself, without moving, in a small Bible study group, one of many which suddenly took shape in the room. The man sitting on his right handed him a booklet opened to the day's lesson. Landon glanced down the titles.

BABYLON IS FALLEN

This was uncanny. He read the references, most of them in Revelation. The discussion opened swiftly, and moved even more swiftly with members of the group sharing what they had learned from reading the passages included in the week's lesson. The teacher, Landon guessed, was a mechanic, for although he was dressed in about the same conservative style as other men in the class, his hands, holding the Bible, were heavily calloused with dark grease lines which had resisted scrubbing.

Everyone seemed to take for granted that Babylon was some Christian church. Which one, Landon could not grasp. Involved in spiritual adultery, which he took to mean unfaithfulness to God.

"If we're all willing to agree that the world is generally rather drunk with the wine of Babylon," the teacher said, "what do you think is the wine of Babylon they have been drinking?"

"False doctrine," said a woman behind Landon.

"Specifically?" A voice to the left one row ahead.

"False Sabbath!" came the same blunt voice behind.

"Pagan ideas." A woman on Landon's left.

"Do you care to elaborate on that?" the teacher asked.

"I'll read it," the woman said. "It's on page 55."

Landon found page 55 in the booklet. He read along.

"This cup of intoxication which she presents to the world represents the false doctrines that she has accepted as the result of her unlawful connection with the great ones of the

103

earth. Friendship with the world corrupts her faith, and in her turn she exerts a corrupting influence upon the world by teaching doctrines which are opposed to the plainest statements of Holy Writ" (*The Great Controversy,* p. 388).

Holy Writ must mean the Bible, Landon guessed. He wished he had brought his Bible, for those around him had theirs open to Revelation 14. He remembered something here.

"Does the call to return to worship of God as creator of heaven and earth have anything to do with this discussion?" he asked. "When I read these chapters recently, I thought of the almost total rejection of the Bible creation story by the modern world."

"False Sabbath," said the voice behind.

"Mark of the Beast," said someone else.

The teacher ran his finger up the column in his Bible.

"You are referring to verse seven," he said. "I'm sure all of you noticed that the wording of this text includes some of the exact phrases used in the fourth commandment in Exodus. Dr. Baines, would you read Exodus 20:8-11? Verse 11 especially."

The man who had given the lesson booklet to Landon read the passage. Landon remembered when he and Robbie and Ryan had read this part in the Bible story book.

"For in six days the Lord made heaven and earth, the sea, and all that in them is, and rested the seventh day: wherefore the Lord blessed the sabbath day, and hallowed it," Dr. Baines read. "So when Christians accept the authority of scientists over the authority of the Bible and adopt a humanistic attitude . . ." Dr. Baines hesitated.

Landon saw the connection he had been looking for. "Then remembering the sabbath of the Old Testament is a sign of your church's belief in God's creative power?"

The teacher nodded. "And in God's re-creative power. We believe that just as God created the world to begin with,

He sustains the order we see in the universe and actively perpetuates life in all living things. Even more wonderful, He provides all that power to rebuild our broken lives if we're willing to give Him the work order."

The doors at the back of the sanctuary opened, and a stream of children came down each of the side aisles. Landon saw Ryan just as Ryan noticed him.

"I guess our discussion ran overtime," the teacher apologized, as members of the class began to leave to collect their children.

All over the room people were regrouping, family members coming from different classes and children joining parents. After a few minutes of organ music, the worship service began. There was a choir at the front, but here congregational music seemed the usual pattern. Landon found the hymn announced. He had never heard it before. The sermon was on forgiveness. Landon kept shifting mentally from the pastor's remarks to the closing remarks of the teacher of the Bible class.

" 'If we confess our sins, He is faithful and just to forgive us our sins, and to cleanse us from all unrighteousness' (1 John 1:9)," the pastor read.

Landon remembered reading that verse.

I know You forgive me, God, Landon thought. *But how do I clear the books with Joetta and Diana?*

Almost in the next breath, the pastor read another passage:

" 'Confess your faults one to another, and pray one for another (James 5:16)."

I was afraid of that, Landon thought. He remembered how his father had made him apologize to Mrs. Johnston after he had stuck out his tongue at her in the store when he was 5. He began to see why a lot of people never went ahead with the "work order" as the class teacher had put it. He was still thinking about that when the organ began the closing song. Ryan reached for the hymnbook and found the page. Landon had heard this song, but he did not sing. Or even try to.

So that's where I go from here, God, he thought. He had been searching for the next step. Now when God pointed it out to him, unmistakably pointed it out, he felt himself drawing back. Well.

In the foyer the dental hygienist found Ryan and introduced herself to Landon.

"How did you like Sabbath School?" she asked Ryan.

"Great!" Ryan said.

They were about to go out the door when the teacher of the Bible class literally ran them down.

"Hold it!" he called, working his way through the crush at the door toward them. "Sorry I didn't have a chance to get acquainted after the lesson study. Sorry we ran over."

"I enjoyed the discussion," Landon said.

"I'm Jim Koblanski."

"Landon Harris."

They shook hands as they moved out of the doorway toward the parking lot. Koblanski was 40 maybe, balding a little, graying a little. Landon could imagine a wrench in the hand which had held the Bible throughout the lesson study.

"Could you have lunch with us?" Koblanski asked. "My wife has invited another family with a couple of kids. We'd enjoy having you."

Landon looked at Ryan.

"Sure. I guess so," he said.

He followed Jim Koblanski through traffic to his home maybe three miles to a new complex of row houses. Grass in front. Grass behind. Snow now, of course. A new version of the kind of neighborhood where he grew up. Nicer. The Koblanskis waited for them at the front door and took their coats once they were inside.

"Yes, diesel engines," Jim said when Landon asked him about his work. "I've been at it since I got out of high school.

Satisfying work. How about yourself?"

"I'm with Hallivand," Landon said. "In engineering."

The other guests were at the door. Jim introduced them while his wife went to the kitchen.

"Calvin's an anesthetist just getting started at Valley Hospital," Jim said. "Ryan, Danny and Sherri know their way around our house. Why don't you let them find something interesting for you to do while the ladies get lunch on the table?"

The children each grabbed one of Ryan's hands and led him up a half level and opened a cabinet.

Landon sat down in the den with Jim and Calvin, men from obviously different backgrounds but also obviously friends.

"Your son was in my Sabbath school class," Calvin said. "He's a real thinker, isn't he?"

Landon felt uneasy.

"Yes," he agreed. "He's good at thinking."

Jim pulled a footstool closer and propped up his feet.

"I'm curious, Landon," he said. "I could see you had studied our lesson today, but I also guessed you are not a Seventh-day Adventist. How did you come to be with us today?"

Landon realized that in all his life he had never had a conversation with other men about religion.

"Actually," he said, "I had not studied your lesson. Only the Bible book of Revelation. I just finished reading it a couple of weeks ago. And, no, I had never met a Seventh-day Adventist before. As Ryan and Robbie put it, we've been 'checking for flavor.' " He explained about visiting different churches over the past several months.

"It's a little unsettling," he said. "That verse about Babylon falling has been hovering around at the edges of my mind for a long time. I dreamed about it this week. Really rather horrible dream complete with sounds and smells."

"I hope the study today was of some help," Jim said.

"You have quite a lively group of students," Landon said.

"You have another son?" Calvin asked.

And Landon found himself explaining things to Jim and Calvin that he had never explained to his own brother. About coping with loneliness. About looking for spiritual help. About finding God and reading the Bible. About guilt and seeking forgiveness.

"I saw quite clearly during the sermon today what God wants me to do," he said. "I guess it's human pride rising up against a direct command. It's going to be hard to ask forgiveness."

"You're right there," Calvin said.

"I keep telling myself that it can only make matters worse. You know the old saying, 'Least said, soonest mended.' "

"Food's ready," called Mrs. Koblanski from the hallway. Calvin rose.

"My mother used to say that, Landon," he said, laying his hand on his arm. "It's often true. But not always. Not where confessing sin is concerned. Nor mending broken hearts."

Mrs. Koblanski had arranged the food along the breakfast bar. After she helped the children fill their plates first, Jim motioned the men to follow. Landon took a plate, filled it, then sat down at the table beside Ryan.

"My dad's a good cook," Ryan told Danny and Sherri. "He makes everything."

"Well, not quite," Landon remarked to Calvin, who was sitting down across from him.

It was nearly 5:00 when they left the Koblanskis.

"Shall we run by the mall for those shoes?" Landon asked Ryan.

"Dad, but it's still Sabbath!" Ryan sounded shocked.

"Well?"

"We can't go shopping on Sabbath," Ryan said. "You know, 'Remember to keep it holy.' "

"Oh."

"Danny said when you keep the Sabbath holy you don't play ball or go shopping or work."

"Oh?" Landon wished he had been able to listen in on the children's conversations at the same time he was involved in the Bible study he had enjoyed with the four adults.

"We'll have to ask Robbie, of course," Ryan went on, "but I told them at Sabbath school as far as I was concerned, we were going to become Seventh-day Adventists. Dad, I asked my teacher about hellfire. He said the same thing you did. Bad people just burn up. Zap! Gone! Not slow sizzle and scorch the way that other preacher said. My teacher said that when everybody has had enough time to make up their minds and God has asked everybody, are they really sure, then GONE! And God starts all over again with everything clean and new like with Adam and Eve. Only everybody already knows about sin this time and isn't curious and can't be fooled. Besides, the devil is burned up too."

"So you like the flavor?"

Ryan pressed his feet out straight ahead against the glovebox. Landon noticed but let him remember for himself.

"They have the facts," Ryan said, dropping his feet.

"You think so?" Landon said. "We'd better give them a full checkout before making up our minds."

When they reached the apartment, Landon mixed some orange juice while Ryan changed his clothes. Ryan came back, took his drink, and headed for the television. He set the juice down and reached to turn on his usual Saturday evening program. He stopped.

"I forgot," he said. "It's Sabbath. We don't watch television on Sabbath."

Landon smiled.

"We don't?"

"Of course not," Ryan said.

Landon had settled in his recliner. He watched Ryan pull out a Bible story book, put it back, then choose another. Ryan drank his juice, leafing through the book until he found the story he wanted. He took his glass and Landon's to the kitchen then climbed onto Landon's lap.

"Dad, did you know these are Seventh-day Adventist books?" Ryan asked.

It's like a puzzle when the major sections begin to take shape, Landon thought. No longer a jumble of unrelated pieces. Still not whole. But beginning to make sense because it was clearly God's hand putting the picture together.

"I'm ready to submit the work order, God," he said under his breath.

PART THREE

ALL DAY Sunday, while he was with Ryan sledding in the park, while they shopped for gym shoes, while he fixed pizza for an early supper, Landon thought about the promise he had made to God during the night. He had spent a long time praying about it, not trying to argue his way out of doing what he knew he must do, but asking for tact, insight. For qualities that he knew from experience he lacked, and needed now more than he had ever needed them before. He had decided he would speak to Diana first. He would return over the bridges in the order he had crossed them. Besides, it would take him longer to fortify himself to tell Joetta what he knew he must say.

Should he write a note? No. That was a cowardly way out. Phone? Maybe. At least to make an appointment. He could hardly charge into her office, which was usually crowded with members of her staff, and ask to speak to her privately. Ringing the doorbell of her new townhouse was even more unthinkable. If Klein were at home—or if he weren't . . .

He called her from work the following morning. He had

thought to ask her to have lunch with him in the cafeteria, but fearing such a public meeting would be the subject of gossip among other Hallivand people, he suggested that she come by his office. Could she set a time convenient for her?

"Directly after lunch Wednesday," she said.

Wednesday she arrived looking anxious.

"Is Ryan all right?" she asked.

"Fine," Landon said. "He's doing just great."

"Sometimes . . ." Diana began. She looked at her nails, glowing like ten perfectly shaped jewels.

"Sit down if you like," Landon said.

She sat down in one of the three chairs facing his desk. She crossed her legs then uncrossed them. Leaned back and then leaned forward.

"Sometimes I think letting you adopt Ryan was the wrong thing to do. Most of the time I know it was best for him. I miss him."

"I'm sorry it's hard for you, Diana," Landon said.

"I'm not the mothering type. It seemed you had more to give him than I did. More of yourself, I mean. You always did. I was always irritated by the amount of time he needed. He always wanted to talk. I don't know how to talk to a kid."

"Sometimes I don't," Landon said. "It's hard being 8 years old. Maybe almost as hard as being 35." How? How should he begin?

"Diana," he said, "I don't want you to think I am trying to get you to rethink the divorce. Both of us know there was nothing solid about our marriage from the beginning. But I realized a few weeks ago that I owe you a thorough apology. And if you'll hear me out, I intend to make it."

"Apology?"

Landon got up from his desk chair and looked out the window. Six stories below the grounds sloped a blinding white in the January sun. The lombardies along the freeway looked dead—like skeleton fingers held up in an effort to hide something but failing.

He spoke, not strong enough to turn to face her.

"Now I realize that you probably knew from the beginning that I never loved you, only became involved with you for the advantage you gave me in my career here at Hallivand. I was such a fool that I believed we were madly in love, that no price was too high to pay for our being together. Then, still more a fool, I thought you had used me for your own career advancement. I became bitter. Blamed you for things I was guilty of myself. Then when you discarded me . . . I felt justified in my judgment. You knew didn't you?"

"Knew what, Landon?"

He turned when she spoke.

"That I loved Joetta all the time. As much as such a selfish man as I could love a wife."

Diana's hands trembled in her lap.

"I think I knew that before you got the divorce from Joetta," she said. "I should have seen . . ."

"I just had to tell you that I'm sorry for whatever unhappiness I've given you. I know it's rather late for me to say so, but . . ."

"At least Ryan has the kind of father he deserves," Diana said. "Are you and Joetta planning to get back together? That would be the best thing in the world for both of the boys."

Landon laughed, the bitterness toward himself rising up like gall in his chest.

"If you were in her place, would you take me back?"

"Probably not. But then, I'm not made out of the same materials Joetta is. She might. She cared a great deal for you once."

Diana rose slowly, then stood erect—beautiful, poised—but a little too much so. She seemed more vulnerable than Landon could remember seeing her. She reminded him of an adolescent girl who had come out first in a sweetheart pageant but wasn't sure anyone really liked her.

"I appreciate your frankness, Landon. You see, it's different with Klein. He really loves me. I didn't snatch him away from anyone. We have a lot in common. He likes the kind of people I like. My kind of entertainment. My family. Do you understand, Landon?"

"I think I do," Landon said. "I'm glad things are working out for you."

"Will you give Ryan my love?"

"I will."

He did. As he drove Ryan home from school that afternoon, he considered how to give the message.

"I saw your mother today at my office," he said.

"Oh?"

Ryan sounded no more interested than if he had mentioned seeing one of the temporary secretaries who occasionally helped him. But Landon noticed that the boy turned suddenly so that he could not see his face.

"She sent you her love," Landon said.

"Did she?" Another sudden movement of his arm to cover his face as he leaned against the car door.

"She says she misses you."

"She's just saying that!" A soft, muffled sob.

Landon looked straight ahead through the traffic.

"No, I think she really does miss you. She may not know how to take care of you, but she still loves you."

"You're just saying that."

Landon wondered how to explain to Ryan what he was beginning to sense about Diana—that her parents had probably given her about the same kind of attention as she had given him—that she didn't really know much about how close and warm a family ought to be.

Obviously Anderson Melton had not informed her of their proposed meeting this week. Just what had the lawyer meant by saying that Ryan was Melton's principal heir? Was

114

Diana's father bypassing her with the bulk of his fortune, or was he cutting out his present wife since she didn't want to bothered with the boy? Maybe he was punishing them both or putting on the pressure to get something he wanted. At this point, Landon didn't want to think about what he was up against. With a father like Melton, how could Diana . . . ?

I should have told her about finding God, he thought. He switched lanes as he approached their exit. *She would have laughed. She would have thought I was being corny. I still should have done it*, he thought. *What Diana really needs is to know that God cares about her. That's what turned me around.*

All evening Ryan was unusually quiet.

"Do you feel like praying?" Landon asked him when he was ready for bed.

"I don't know how," Ryan said in a trembling voice.

"I'm not too good at it myself, but I've been practicing," Landon said. "I guess God doesn't mind."

"I guess not."

Landon could see that Ryan felt awkward kneeling beside his bed. The boy glanced at him swiftly then closed his eyes.

"God, we really do want to learn how to live the way You want us to," Landon began. "Most of the time we are confused and feel pretty bad about the way things get messed up. We're sorry. We know You love us, and we love You. God, we need some help to understand how we ought to try to patch up the messes. Ryan feels bad about his mother. So do I. We wish we could learn how to forgive the way You have forgiven us."

He felt Ryan shift, and all at once the boy's arms were around his neck. Landon rocked back on his heels and held Ryan close. Both of them cried. Finally Landon tucked Ryan under the covers and lay down beside him, his arm resting over the child until he fell asleep. Then he rose carefully and went to his study. He found the Bible lesson booklet Dr.

Baines had given him in church on Saturday. He went to the den and sat down with it.

"He that saith, I know him, and keepeth not his commandments, is a liar, and the truth is not in him. But whoso keepeth his word, in him verily is the love of God perfected: hereby know we that we are in him" (1 John 2:4, 5).

Landon read the memory text and thought about it. He scanned the portions of the lesson which followed but found most of the information to be based on some historic events he knew nothing about. He came across one Bible verse which reinforced the first.

"Here is the patience of the saints: here are they that keep the commandments of God and the faith of Jesus" (Rev. 14:12).

I need patience, he thought. *I need to have the love of God perfected in me.*

"Please, God. Do it."

He remembered learning to swim with his mother's arms under him. He remembered thrashing wildly to make his body surge ahead in the water—his mother walking along with him, always there with support. But she let him struggle and learn how.

I've got that to remember, he thought. *Ryan doesn't.*

But he has me. "God, if You keep backing me up, I can do that for him."

Although it was nearly 10:00, Landon called Joetta. As he dialed the number, all the openings he had rehearsed seemed contrived, shoddy.

"Joetta, I need to talk to you," he said. "Something wonderful has happened. I mean, God has forgiven me, and now I'm asking your forgiveness. I . . ." All at once he realized how little sense he was making. "I'm sorry, Joetta," he said. "I do need to talk to you."

"Landon?" He heard Joetta draw her breath, waiting for him to go on. He thought she sounded irritated.

116

"I'm sorry," he said. "You have no way to know where I'm coming from. This afternoon I cleared my accounts with Diana. I mean, I made my apologies—acknowledged I've been wrong." He hesitated. "I've been even more wrong in the way I've treated you. Maybe you can't forgive, but at least I have to tell you that I recognize everything was my fault. At least I have to say I'm sorry."

"Don't you think that's a pretty feeble excuse for all . . . ?"

"Yes, I do. Very feeble. And it doesn't make up for anything. Joetta, I'm not asking . . ."

He couldn't finish. He knew that she knew he was indeed asking more than for a blanket forgiveness for the past.

"I didn't mean to take the easy out on the telephone," he said. "I meant to ask you and Robbie to go to church with Ryan and me. I was hoping you would see . . ."

"Landon." Joetta's voice was definitely strained. "So you've decided to try religion. How am I supposed to take that? Am I supposed to . . . ?"

She did not finish although he waited.

Landon drew squares inside of squares on his notepad.

"I'm willing to admit that some things, once they're broken, can never be put back together," he said. "Trust. Marriage. Home. I'm not asking for you to believe you can trust me again. Just believe I'm sorry."

"I believe you," she said. "Good night, Landon."

He held the phone after she hung up, the dial tone buzzing in his ear. Strange that while he felt intense pain he also sensed infinite relief. He set the phone down and rested his face in his hands.

"What next, God? I did what You said. I'm ready for the next step as soon as You tell me what it is."

Anderson Melton's lawyer and a secretary were seated at the table in the private conference room off Melton's inner office when Landon arrived at his former father-in-law's downtown suite on Tuesday. The lawyer indicated a chair to Landon just as Melton came in the door.

"I suppose you know—I suppose Phelps has told you—that in reviewing my will I realized that changes would need to be made to accommodate Ryan's inheritance as well as the trust funds already in his name. Mr. Phelps can present the details of things as they stand and suggest changes that seem necessary under the circumstances."

"I did not realize that you had designated Ryan as an heir inasmuch as his mother has proposed I adopt him. I assumed that any claims he might have as your grandson would be relinquished when the adoption becomes final."

Melton snorted. "Quite the contrary. As long as Diana made some show of accepting her responsibility toward the boy, I went along with her. But since she wants to be a playgirl, let her play. This Klein she's in with has big ideas about helping me invest a few million. Showed his hand a little too soon. Diana's marital affairs may be outside my control, but Ryan is still Melton bone and blood, whatever name he carries. Phelps, explain the conditions to Landon. Give me 15 minutes. I have a client on the phone."

It was really quite simple. According to the documents on the table, Ryan would assume control of half the Melton fortune at the age of 30. Until then sums would be made available at appropriate times for travel or advanced education. During his minority he was to receive a monthly allowance of $5,000 to be used at Landon's discretion. At the age of 21 Ryan would receive certain properties designated by his grandfather if at that time Melton was satisfied that he was prepared to manage them.

"So where are the strings?" Landon asked when Phelps finished.

The lawyer glanced at him sharply, then acknowledged Melton, who had returned.

"Mr. Melton insists that under no circumstances will you

118

become reconciled to his daughter, and under no circumstances will you agree to allow her to regain control of his grandson."

"I'm sure she doesn't want me back," Landon told Melton.

"She might when she receives a copy of these documents," Melton said.

Color flooded the older man's face. He walked around the table, then dropped into his chair and pounded with both fists at once. "I'll not let her get the best of me in this one!"

Phelps stacked the papers. Landon noticed the look which passed between the lawyer and the secretary.

"I don't want any part of this family fight," Landon said.

"Sorry about that," Melton said, his voice rising. "If you want the boy, you'll have to consider my point of view. While I believe Ryan is better off with you than with me, I'm not about to give you a totally free hand. Do you want him? I demand an agreement that Diana will have no further authority where he is concerned. That's only sensible."

"Yes," Landon said.

He signed.

Had he done the right thing? Or had he capitulated to a bribe? In his own mind, Landon was satisfied that $5,000 a month was no consideration, that even the long term inheritance was not important to him or to Ryan. Yet, everyone wouldn't see things that way. Diana for one. Melton's current wife for another. What really mattered was settling the adoption. And if Melton meant to see that his wife did not get his money, he might in a showdown put his loyalty to Ryan over his relationship with her.

Landon looked at the situation from every angle he could imagine. He called his lawyer and listened to his reassurances.

"So what are you kicking about? You get the boy. You

get $5,000 a month to help pay his bills. No worries about university or sports cars. And what are you giving up? Nothing."

"Possibly my integrity."

While Ryan designed a magnificent skyscraper of interlocking blocks that evening, Landon wondered just what areas of their lives Melton would try to manipulate in the future.

"Are You still there in charge," he prayed after Ryan was asleep. "I'm trying to do things Your way. I'm not sure about signing. It seemed the only way."

They picked Robbie up at the after-hours program at his school on Friday.

"Mom's busy with a meeting," he told Ryan. "She has meetings all day tomorrow too. She's trying out for a new job."

"We're going to Sabbath school tomorrow," Ryan said. "You know, like Sunday school, only on Saturday." And he launched into an account of their visit to the Seventh-day Adventist church that lasted until they reached the apartment.

Landon made a quick supper of burgers and fries for the boys.

"There's a real neat show on TV tonight," Robbie said, dipping a potato in his catsup. "It comes on at 7:00."

"Oh, no!" Ryan burst in. "We can't watch TV tonight. It's already Sabbath. Isn't it, Dad?"

Robbie put that fry into his mouth and began stirring in the catsup with another while Ryan went on about proper ways to spend the time on Sabbath. Evidently Danny and Sherri had been very thorough in the instruction they gave Ryan the Saturday before.

"It's a good show, Dad," Robbie said when Ryan stopped long enough to take a big bite out of his burger.

"What kind of program is it?" Landon asked.

"How come he's all of a sudden so excited about the Bible?" Robbie asked. "Ryan, I thought you were mad at God. I thought you thought we were stupid going to church."

"You just have to come to Sabbath school tomorrow. You'll see," Ryan said. He took another deep bite into his burger. "Won't he, Dad?"

Landon grinned. "I think Ryan enjoyed Sabbath school," he said, winking at Robbie.

"You did too."

"You're right, Ryan. I did. Very much."

Landon half expected an argument about the TV program, but none developed. When he had loaded the dishwasher and washed the ketchup from the table, he found the boys sprawled on the floor in the den with the Bible story book open to the Ten Commandments. Robbie had his felt markers and a drawing pad and was making his own copy of the tables of stone engraved with his own careful printing.

Although they set out early the next morning, the roads were slick, and they arrived at the church late. When they entered, the receptionist offered to take Ryan and Robbie to their classroom.

"Oh, I know the way," Ryan insisted and set off with Robbie down a side hallway.

Landon nodded to the host and went in to sit down in the same place where he had sat last week. Dr. Baines, seated farther to the right, signed "hello" just as the lights went out and a slide presentation began.

"This is Mission Spotlight," announced a heavy bass voice. Iceland was the subject—Seventh-day Adventist work in Iceland.

Later the Sabbath school leader pointed out the figures on the back of the lesson booklet. Landon compared the Adventist membership in various European nations on the map to total population. While membership was not large, it seemed that the church did have a significant presence in each of the nations pictured, and from what Jim Koblanski had said last week, he guessed that the church was a global one.

He was hardly better prepared now to follow this lesson study than the last, for he had become bogged down with the "beast," the "image to the beast," and the "mark of the beast." As the class discussion progressed, he became more confused than ever. Jim was already glancing apprehensively at his watch when he introduced his final question.

"Last week we talked about the world being drunk with the 'wine of Babylon.' Now let's take a look at the 'wine of the wrath of God.' Just what is it? What about the fire and brimstone? How long does it take for God's wrath to burn itself out?"

Glancing at his lesson booklet, Landon noticed this section for the first time, along with several Bible references.

"God's wrath lasts only until sin is consumed," said Dr. Baines.

"Until all the wicked are nothing but a heap of ashes," said a lady two rows back.

"Malachi 4:3," added a very positive voice to the left.

Here the children began streaming into the sanctuary.

"I'm sorry," Jim said. "We never seem to finish the lesson, do we? Landon, since you have your Bible open to Revelation 14, would you read verse 12?"

Landon's eyes dropped down to the verse.

"Here is the patience of the saints: here are they that keep the commandments of God and have the faith of Jesus," he read. He felt rather over-dosed with information.

The class members started moving out of the pew. Ryan and Robbie waited for Dr. Baines to leave then sat down beside Landon.

"So this is your brother?" Jim said, to Ryan. "So you're Robbie?"

He reached to shake Landon's hand. "Plan to stay after the sermon. We're having a potluck today."

Ushers passed out printed announcements of an upcoming event while someone spoke from the pulpit about plans and congregational involvement in the event. Landon took the leaflet handed him and slipped it into his Bible.

"Hey, Dad," Robbie whispered. "That's the man you used to watch on TV last year."

Landon looked at the picture on Robbie's leaflet. He was right. The evangelist pictured was the same one who preached the "Babylon Is Fallen" sermon at the beginning of May. Another piece of the puzzle fell into its place. He was thinking about that as the speaker began the sermon a few minutes later. The preacher read a text in Second Peter about being partakers of the divine nature. Landon noticed when he found the place that he had jotted a note in the margin when he read this verse a few weeks earlier. Jeremiah 31:33-34. Funny how the Bible all tied together so wonderfully. But then, not strange really since God was in charge of the whole thing from first to last. Landon mused about how he had heard God's voice speaking to him as he read Jeremiah that first night when he decided to accept God as his Father. That same voice had spoken to him all the way through the New Testament, even when he found more information than he could assimilate at once, like today.

In the foyer after church Landon moved with the crowd down the hall, presumably toward the potluck dinner. He hadn't been to a potluck since he was a kid when his mother took a covered dish to PTA suppers. Calvin and his wife came up behind him.

"I wish I had known. I could have brought something," Landon said.

"Think nothing of it," Calvin said. "There's always more than everyone can eat."

Danny and Sherri, along with three of their friends had surrounded Ryan and Robbie.

"Ryan was really impressed with your explanation of hellfire," Landon told Calvin. "You'll have to give me the whole picture along with the Bible references. Ryan's account was rather colorful. 'Sizzle! Zap!' I believe was how he put it."

The dinner was already spread on six long tables in what appeared to be a gymnasium. In a few minutes, by some kind of signal, the room was suddenly quiet, and the minister gave a prayer of thanks for the food. Landon was halfway down the service table, his plate already filled, when he realized there was no meat. None whatever. There must be some explanation. He wondered.

Well.

When Landon took Robbie back to Joetta's on Sunday evening, he did not mention their telephone conversation the previous Wednesday. He had stepped into her apartment while Robbie showed Ryan something in his room.

"Robbie tells me you are thinking about a new position at the university," he said.

Joetta sat across the room from him on the arm of the sofa.

"Actually it's not so much a new job. I was taking qualifying exams for a grant. It's possible that I might be able to complete a Ph.D. in less than two years if I get this financial backing."

"I didn't know you have been doing graduate work," Landon said.

"It's been slow when I've worked full time," Joetta said, touching her shoe to the coffee table's corner. "If I get the grant, the university will give me a leave of absence from my position without a lapse in benefits. When the degree is completed, I will be in line for an opening that is due to come in the dean's office. I've been grooming for that spot for quite a while."

Landon heard the boys move from Robbie's room to the kitchen, the refrigerator door open and close.

"How are you planning to manage with Robbie while you have such a heavy study load?"

Joetta stepped to the kitchen door.

"Robbie, get Ryan some crackers to go with the milk," she said. She came back and sat down. "I had hoped Mother would be willing to come live with us until I get most of my library work completed. But even though she is eligible for retirement, she wants to keep on with her job. And she is really uncomfortable in the city. You know."

"Of course."

He could see the boys through the doorway, leaning against the counter drinking milk and dipping crackers in a carton of cheese spread.

"Maybe I could have him with me during the week and you could have him weekends," he suggested. "It might work out better that way temporarily." He watched for her reaction. "If you . . ."

"I don't know," she said too quickly.

"I'm not trying to . . ."

"I know, but . . ."

Peggy showed up at his office the following week. Very charming. Very concerned.

"I hope you see that Ryan doesn't get chilled in this awful weather," she said.

"He's doing fine," Landon said.

"I worry about him."

"He's doing fine," Landon repeated. "I make him wear longjohns to school in case they play outdoors."

"Are you sure . . . ?"

"Look, Peggy," Landon told her. "I realize that I might

not have all the motherly instincts a woman has, but we're doing fine. Right now I'm up against a demanding work schedule."

But she was persistent. Twice more during January she came by on one pretext or another. Landon guessed her mother had the information about Ryan's inheritance and Peggy was trying to lay claim to part of it. He wished the adoption was settled.

During February Chicago froze and thawed by turn, its citizens wallowing in snowstorms, then wading through slush as the snow melted. Landon's work at Hallivand was like the weather; sometimes he was caught in a rush of cross currents, sometimes knee-deep in deliberations. He and Ryan occasionally spent an evening at the library or at a mall, but they were used to outdoor activities, and with the skating rink in the park a mass of ridges and hollows and the children's ski slope either bare or glazed over, they were driven indoors. Twice Landon had gone to the athletic club to which he belonged, but since he had to find a sitter for Ryan, he felt uneasy about that. Some evenings they watched television.

But Landon had never been strong on TV, and Ryan was less interested than he used to be.

"If we weren't swallowed up in the city, I'd say I had cabin fever," he told Reynolds one day at work.

Much of his unrest, Landon knew, was the result of his uncertainties about the future. He kept expecting to hear from Diana. Or the social worker in charge of the case. Maybe it was just as well he hadn't brought up religion when he talked with Diana. It was just as well Melton didn't know he was taking the boy to church. Somehow Landon had the feeling Melton would try to dictate quite a few things if he had the chance. Landon tried to shrug off his worries.

The more time he spent with his new friends at the Seventh-day Adventist church, the more he was drawn into their lifestyle. He liked the easy camaraderie among members, the informal, yet reverent attitude in their church services, the total confidence in the Bible as the literal Word of God. It seemed too good to be real. It seemed to Landon that something so good could hardly be the property of such an insignificant group. Why, until he visited the church for the first time, he had never noticed the name Seventh-day Adventist.

In some ways, being with the church group was like stepping back in time—into more wholesome times with more wholesome values. And yet, neither the Koblanskis nor their friends really seemed old-fashioned. It was just their value system, which reminded him of the values his parents had cherished, even if they had not been churchgoers.

"Don't hang your confidence on me," Jim Koblanski had warned him. "I'm going to do everything I can, by the grace of God, to be a good example of what God wants a man to be. But I'm very likely to fall myself, since I'm made out of the same kind of human flesh you are, Landon. Keep your eyes on Jesus."

Landon noticed that Calvin and his wife had discipline problems with Danny and Sherri, that parents of teenagers at church often had the same kind of conflicts with their children that most parents have. There were members who had been divorced. Being a Seventh-day Adventist did not guarantee peace and harmony.

"Becoming a member of the church does not cancel your freedom of choice," Jim said. "And since within the church we are still free to make choices, we sometimes make wrong ones. We expect to grow more like Jesus the longer we walk with Him. And through His grace we expect to beat the sin habit. Giving your life to Jesus is something you can do in a minute. Becoming like Him is a lifetime proposition. You are always free to change your mind if you're dissatisfied."

Ryan already considered himself to be a Seventh-day

Adventist—had told his friends at school that he was. Robbie, on the other hand, had mixed loyalties. There was his grandmother's church in Waterford where his mother had grown up a part of the church family. And here in the city there was the large church where Joetta took him and where he had made friends in the Sunday school. What his teacher there told him and what the preacher preached did not always agree with what he heard at the Adventist church when he attended with Landon. Landon could see that in both churches he had become a resistant listener. The Bible story books, which Grandma Smith had bought him, remained solid ground for him, a part of both situations.

The Adventist churches in Chicago sponsored a large evangelistic campaign bridging between February and March. Landon attended most of the meetings but left early in order to get Ryan to bed. The chief value of the series was that he began to see how the book of Daniel in the Old Testament and the book of Revelation in the New Testament provided a sensible framework for understanding prophesies throughout the Bible. While he had never been a history buff, he knew where to find reference books in which he could verify the historical information the evangelist presented in his sermons. Now, instead of being a nightmarish collection of symbols of disaster, the book of Revelation became a comprehensible outline of real events, past, present, and future. Landon began to see how the return of Jesus promised in Revelation was a reality described throughout the Bible and how Jesus' return, not the destruction of the world, was the event of all events to which believers could look forward.

By the end of the evangelistic meetings Landon had made numerous private commitments and a few public ones. But he had not decided to join the Adventist Church. He did not request baptism although he saw that Jim and some of his other church friends had hoped he would.

I'm waiting for the adoption to go through, he admitted to himself, ashamed in the admission of the fact.

It was not the individual doctrines of the church which created a barrier. All the way, he had accepted the plain Bible truth each time a new subject was presented. The problem was a mixture of fear about his own ability to carry through with so total a commitment to such a radically different religious orientation. In a way he worried about how Anderson Melton would take such a change. And to be honest, he worried how Joetta would take it.

Landon had not spoken to Joetta again about his conversion. In fact, he had spoken to her very little about anything.

She invited Landon to come for Robbie's birthday party the second week in March, a party to which she had invited a half dozen children—two of Robbie's friends from school, Danny and Sherri from the Adventist church, and one boy from Robbie's Sunday school.

"I received the grant," Joetta told him. "I begin my leave of absence the first of May."

"Great," Landon congratulated her.

"I've decided that at least for the summer we should try Robbie spending five days a week with you if you still want to. When his school term begins in the fall, we'll probably have to arrange something else."

"We'll go camping lots this summer. Won't we, Dad?" Robbie said as soon as he heard about their plans.

"When shall I take my vacation?" Landon asked the boys. "Where shall we go?"

"We've been reading the book we bought you," Ryan said. "Somewhere wild—really wild. We want to be like explorers."

"How about Canada?" Landon had dreamed of a vacation in the Canadian wilderness when he was a boy, but his parents could never afford more than a couple of days at a state park nearby.

They began making plans and buying camping equipment. Joetta OK'd the idea. Landon asked for three weeks off in July.

"We'd better buy a canoe," Robbie said.

"Let's just rent one," Landon said. "Where would we keep a canoe here?"

Robbie grinned. "Grandma Smith would let us keep it in her garage, and we could go up there sometimes and practice in the river. We're going to have to build up our muscles."

"He's right," Ryan agreed. "We need practice."

The ice was just breaking up on Lake Michigan when they found the canoe and trailer. But it was May before they got it into the water on the river at Waterford. On their first trip there, Landon checked into a motel. They got up early in the morning and spent the whole day on the river, stopping only for lunch at a public picnic area.

"Let me know when you're coming next time," Mrs. Smith said when they parked the canoe and trailer in her large garage that evening. "There's no sense in your renting a room when I'm here alone in this big house. Besides, I'll enjoy having the boys with me."

Through May, Robbie was with them every weekend since Joetta had begun her library research and needed Saturdays to study. Three times Landon took Ryan and Robbie to Waterford, driving up on a Saturday afternoon and spending the night with Grandma Smith.

"I've never quite given you up, Landon," she said once as she fed him breakfast. "Every woman needs a son."

Landon remembered what Joetta had told him about her brother when they were first married. He was not a bad boy, she said, just terribly independent. Impatient with their parents' quiet ways and old-fashioned values. They had tried to find him right after he ran away. For two or three years—but had finally decided that he was determined not to be found.

She's still grieving for him, Landon thought. He watched her filling his plate with French toast at the stove. He was startled when she looked up. The expression in her eyes.

She's still grieving for me, he thought, taking the plate and pouring syrup over the toast. He felt his throat tightening. This was part of what he had thrown away when he left Joetta. Here was one more pain he had inflicted.

"I wish . . ." Mrs. Smith began. She heard the boys on the stairs and did not finish.

I wish too, Landon thought. *Oh, how I wish.*

"I wish Mom could go canoeing with us," Robbie said, coming into the kitchen. "She likes to go in a motorboat, but this is lots better. Grandma, last time we came right up on this muskrat. He was right in front of us! This close!" He measured perhaps 18 inches between his hands.

"Why don't you ask her to come up some Sunday soon?" Mrs. Smith suggested, looking over Robbie's head at Landon. "It would be good for her to get away from her research and get some fresh air."

"Yes, let's ask her," Ryan agreed.

Landon was sure the boys would ask her, and he half hoped for, half dreaded the outcome. She would probably think he had worked on her mother, trying to take advantage of her need for help with Robbie.

During a sermon in June, Landon came to what he knew must be his time of decision. The pastor told the story of how God called the patriarch Abraham to sacrifice his son to prove his loyalty. At that moment, as the pastor described the old man's anguish, Landon knew what was holding him back. He was afraid to follow his convictions because if he did he might lose Ryan or Robbie—possibly both of them. Melton might accept Ryan's being raised in a fashionable church, but hardly in the Seventh-day Adventist Church.

And if he became a Seventh-day Adventist, would Joetta try to cut the time he had Robbie with him? Would joining the church close the door to all hope that they might get back together?

"Until I'm willing to go ahead regardless of the consequences, I'm not really entirely Your man, am I, Father?" he prayed while the pastor began an altar call at the end of the sermon.

He stood in silence, his head bowed, listening to one pair of feet moving softly down the carpeted center aisle toward the pastor. *I'm going,* he decided. "Yes, Father, I'm giving You my boys. Oh, keep us all together! Please!"

He turned toward the center, opening his eyes at the end of the pew, his eyes drawn to the pastor. It was then he saw Ryan standing next to the pastor, his head bowed. Landon rushed toward him, reaching to grip the pastor's hand even as he reached with the other arm to circle his son.

At that moment he realized that whatever complications might be ahead for them, God would certainly settle matters for them if they were willing to commit themselves to Him.

"I knew you would come if I went first," Ryan told him as they drove home that day. "I've prayed for a long time, Dad. The pastor told me I was too young to be baptized, so I decided the only thing to do was to help you make up your mind."

"Everything is going to be all right," Landon told himself repeatedly during the days that followed.

Ryan's adoption finally went through the Friday before Landon was baptized, and they felt like a celebration, and since Ryan had spread the word in his Sabbath school class, the fellowship dinner after church became a party.

"Double adoption," Jim Koblanski said. "Now Ryan belongs to you, and both of you belong to us!"

While he wasn't entirely satisfied with the arrangement, Landon enrolled both Ryan and Robbie in a summer day care program which included crafts and outdoor recreation as well as "educational enrichment." The center was located conveniently so that he could take the boys as he went to work and pick them up as he came home—actually a major consideration when he decided.

He soon discovered that when the boys spent more time together, they generated more friction between them— more like natural brothers, he supposed, remembering how he and Tom had quarrelled over a shared room, how he and Mary had yelled at each other and fought over possessions.

At a ball game in which both boys played Landon stood with other fathers and sons waiting for their uniforms. Landon fell into conversation with a man with whom he had worked briefly at Hallivand during the winter.

"Which of these boys is your real son?" the man asked.

Landon caught the look that passed between Ryan and Robbie.

"They both are," Landon said.

"But I thought . . ." the man began.

"They are both mine," Landon said.

"Are we?" Ryan asked as they drove home when the game was over.

"Of course, you are?" Landon said. "I've adopted you. Signed and sealed. And Robbie has always been my son."

But occasionally he overheard bits of their conversations.

"I've lived with Dad all the time since I was just a little kid."

"Well, I was with him when I was a baby. Mom showed me the picture of when I was first born."

"Dad won't like that. I know better than you what Dad likes."

"Well, you have another father somewhere."

"No, I don't. Dad's my dad."

Instead of rivalry over bikes and baseball bats or closet

133

space, Robbie and Ryan had fallen into competition over their father.

And over their mother. More precisely over Joetta. Months ago Joetta had told Landon that she expected to treat Ryan just as she treated Robbie's other friends, but it was clear that Ryan hungered for the same kind of mothering she gave Robbie. Landon noticed the expression which crossed his face whenever Robbie said in his very possessive way, "My mom."

Mrs. Smith overheard one of their discussions at her house.

"Robbie," she said, "if Ryan is your brother, I am his grandma as well as yours. Not sort of. Really, truly. One hundred percent."

That seemed to settle the grandmother issue. On the surface at least.

Joetta agreed to join them at her mother's for canoeing the second weekend in June.

"I know this will seem strange to you," Landon told her on the phone when they made plans. "And it hardly seems fair considering that you usually attend church on Sunday. But I've come to have some pretty strong convictions about keeping Saturday as the Sabbath. Do you mind if we spend Sunday, not Saturday on the river?"

"I'll have to study Saturday anyway, even if I'm at Mother's," Joetta said. "Just drive up after you attend church. We'll play it by ear from there."

"I have something personal that I'd like all of you to pray about," Landon told his Sabbath school class. "I don't feel free to talk about it publicly, but I know that all of you are concerned about me and my family. I don't know what God wants to do for us, so I guess it really doesn't matter if you don't know exactly what the situation is. Just pray for us. For me. I know what I want. I need to be willing to accept what God sees is best for us."

Landon arrived at Waterford about 4:00.

Joetta was with her mother on the side porch, a pile of photocopies in her lap and a loose-leaf notebook open on a table beside her.

"Hi, Mom!" Robbie shouted, running to hug her.

"Hello," Ryan said. "Hi, Grandma!" He hugged Mrs. Smith and then squeezed Joetta's hand as she reached around Robbie to him.

"I've planned supper in the park," Mrs. Smith said.

"We brought a watermelon. It's in the ice chest—nice and cold," Ryan told her. Landon leaned against the railing.

In a few minutes Mrs. Smith took the boys inside to show them something.

"So you've become a Seventh-day Adventist?" Joetta said, gathering her paperwork together then stretching in her chair, raising her feet and drawing circles in the air with her tennis shoes.

"Yes," Landon said. "I was baptized less than a month ago."

"Oh, I thought you had joined them months ago."

He moved to the seat her mother had just left.

"I guess I've been overly cautious. I didn't want to rush into something I might change my mind about later."

Joetta set her feet down and leaned forward.

"Oh?"

"I wanted to have everything solid—to understand fully what I'm promising to do before I committed myself." Landon tried to pinpoint exactly what he did mean. "I made a firm decision about being a Christian months ago. I turned my life over to God without any reservations. Except that letting Him work out all the complications is a little scary. I knew He was leading me to become an Adventist, but I was afraid of the consequences."

"They're good people," Joetta said. "I've worked with one for several years. Do you remember Betty? The gray-haired lady who used to be receptionist in the front office. And

135

we've had quite a few doctoral candidates who took earlier work at the Adventist university. It's just a few miles from here, you know."

"No, I didn't know," Landon said.

"Robbie seems to enjoy the children's activities at the Adventist church," Joetta said. "He's even talked about attending their elementary school next year."

Landon laughed. "Ryan has too. How do you suppose a teacher would feel about having both of them in her room? Would you believe I've found out a few things about parenting in the past two weeks?"

"Ready to head for the park?" called Mrs. Smith from inside.

Landon carried the ice chest while the boys each toted a paper sack.

It was nearly dark when they loaded the remains of the picnic into the car and drove back to Mrs. Smith's house.

"Grandma bought us another book," Ryan said when he and Robbie had dressed for bed. "Will you read it for worship, Dad?"

Landon took the book and sat on the floor in front of the sofa with one boy on either side leaning against him and opened the book. It was the story of the life of Christ, beautifully illustrated. He was about to start at the beginning, but Ryan reached to open to a place where he had inserted a scrap of paper.

"This one, Dad," he said.

It was the story of the prodigal son.

When he closed the book after the story, the boys looked at him as if asking why they didn't kneel to pray. Embarrassed, but recognizing that prayer was something that would be appropriate in this house, he said, "Do you ladies care to pray with us?"

At home they knelt in a tight circle with their arms around each other's shoulders. Now, with his arm around

Robbie, he felt his hand brush against Joetta's sleeve, and he was instantly aware how much he wanted to hold her, to tell her he needed her for himself as well as for the boys. Both boys prayed, then Mrs. Smith. Landon hardly trusted himself to speak.

"Heavenly Father, we thank You for loving us. We love You too," he prayed.

"I hope you two will excuse me if I have to study for a couple more hours," Joetta said when Landon came back from settling the boys in bed.

"I'll help your mother in the kitchen," he said.

At the river in the morning Landon rented a second canoe and more life vests. Joetta, her mother, and Robbie got into the rented canoe while Ryan and Landon packed the food and extra gear into theirs.

"We're getting in shape, aren't we, Grandma?" Robbie asked as they set out upstream.

"You're putting a lot of power into your strokes," Joetta told him from the stern. "You'll do just fine when you get to Canada."

With the two canoes moving side by side, the boys told Joetta and Mrs. Smith about their maps and the wildlife they expected to see on their vacation.

"You might see some on this river today," Joetta said. "I remember seeing a doe with a fawn once."

Landon remembered too. The first trip he had made to Waterford—the time he came to meet her parents when he and Joetta started serious dating. He remembered paddling up along the bank, evading the strongest current, remembered Joetta showing him places she and her father liked to explore—a small stream they had followed more than a mile between brushy banks, then open woods, and finally to a meadow with farm buildings off in the distance. He remembered how the doe stood with her head down to the water, her ears rotating in the most amazing way. He remembered the fawn's tail fluttering, his skin twitching as if a fly might be tickling his spotted side. That was the day he first realized he loved Joetta. She remembered.

Mrs. Smith noticed the muskrat first. All of them stopped talking, but they kept on paddling since they were going upstream. The muskrat saw them, turned a little to the right, but kept swimming downstream as if he were on very important business.

"He's going home," Ryan whispered after he passed them. "See, he's in a hurry." He turned in his seat to watch the small brown head moving steadily away with silver ripples moving out from the widening V behind it.

And they saw dozens of frogs, possibly a dozen turtles.

Robbie and Joetta had been in the lead, but Landon eased ahead of them. Not certain until he reached the spot, he turned his canoe into a marshy area, threading his way along the narrow creek that came into the river here.

"This is neat," Robbie said from the bow of the other canoe, now almost nudging Landon's. "This is almost wilderness."

"I'm glad I put on insect repellant," commented Mrs. Smith. "I hear the mosquitoes singing."

Alders and brushy willows pressed in from both sides. The stream meandered.

"No turning back from here," Landon laughed. "Not unless you want to drift back to the river in reverse." If he remembered correctly, they would soon come out into more open territory with pines on higher ground.

Instead, they came suddenly upon a dam with a beaver pond above it, the water dancing with dragonflies.

"Will the beavers be mad at us if we use their pond, Dad?" Robbie asked in a whisper again.

"Shall we?" Landon asked Joetta.

"Why not?" she said.

Landon stepped out on a log and pulled his canoe close enough for Ryan to get out. He drew it up on the grassy bank then pulled Joetta's canoe up. Hardly whispering, they walked the canoes around the end of the dam and launched them silently into the water on the pond.

The boys, who had been paddling bow, did not take up their paddles but sat motionless while Landon and Joetta took long deep strokes, moving the canoes forward without so much as the drip of water from their paddles. Robbie saw a great blue heron and pointed. A pair of mallards followed by seven ducklings swam along the shore, first in the shade of overhanging bushes, then in full sunlight not 30 feet away.

Landon smiled at Ryan's efforts to contain his excitement.

He directed the canoe to where the pond narrowed again to a streambed that was mossy on one side, rocky on the other—between pines much larger than he had remembered.

It's been 17 years, he thought. *If this is really the same place.*

"This looks like a good spot for a picnic," Joetta said. "Is anybody else hungry?"

And all at once their dammed-up chatter broke loose.

"Hungry enough to eat a bear!"

"Did you count those little ducks?"

"Mom, did you see where the beavers cut the trees for their house?"

"I want some lemonade."

Joetta and her mother spread a blanket on the pine needles in the shade and brought out sandwiches and potato salad from the ice chest.

"Olives! Did you bring olives, Grandma?" Robbie asked between gulps of lemonade.

Landon felt a deep silence building inside him as if he could stand here, his back pressed against the rough pine bark listening forever, as if he had nothing whatever to say but only a powerful need to absorb all the meaning from each word the boys said, each word Joetta said, as if somehow he could unscramble from their unguarded statements of pleasure what he needed to know about them and about himself.

He ate his chips and carrot sticks, potato salad and olives, savoring the flavors, the textures of each mouthful as if he had never tasted these foods before. He rested his shoulders flat against the tree and drew in his breath.

I'm hardly a hundred miles from Hallivand, he thought absently.

He was surprised to see Joetta standing beside him, a sandwich in her hand.

"Want another one?"

Their eyes met for an instant before Landon reached to take it. Their eyes met again when he looked up.

"Life won't always be this idyllic," Joetta said.

"Are you willing to try again?" Landon whispered.

If you enjoyed this book, you'll want to read these other best-sellers.

April Showers, by VeraLee Wiggins. When Eric walks out on April, leaving her with three tiny children, tremendous bills, and no way to make a decent income, she doesn't have the slightest idea how to manage on her own. But as the months pass, her grief turns to anger, then action. Determined to get off welfare and make a happy life for her family, she goes back to school. Along the way she discovers a genuine friend in her heavenly Father and an unexpected romance. Paper, 125 pages. US$7.95, Cdn$9.95.

Jenny's Song, by VeraLee Wiggins. Jenny had been in love from the moment she had laid eyes on Fletch Leighton. And sometimes his eyes let her know he cared—but then the reserved coolness would return. It wasn't until Jenny learned to love the Lord that she understood. Paper, 128 pages. US$7.95, Cdn$9.95.

Jump the Wind, by Sandra Bandy. At age 14 the author stepped forward at an evangelistic meeting. Then her parents forbade her attending the Seventh-day Adventist church. Feeling cut off from the God she had just met, she drifted into drugs and eventually mental illness. But God was there, ready to calm the storm in her life. Paper, 128 pages. US$7.95, Cdn$9.95.

Logan's Wife, by Minita Sype Brown and Rosalie Hunt Mellor. Elusive dreams beckoned Logan, constantly uprooting Minnie from the things she loved. But each time she moved, this courageous woman found a way to share God's love with those around her. Paper, 96 pages. US$6.95, Cdn$8.70.

Shattered Dreams, by VeraLee Wiggins. It was a happy marriage. Then Judd stunned Amy by abandoning his goal of becoming a pastor. Angry and disillusioned with religion, he pleaded with Amy to follow him rather than God. Which would she sacrifice,

her conscience or her marriage . . . or both? Paper, 128 pages.
US$7.95, Cdn$9.95.
